"Strong themes of self-reflection and discovery unfold through the eyes of Hannah Skye and her aunt, Jewelia, hosting a celebration to honor the 999 portal's opening. Mary delivers rich fantasy and an engaging mystery. The unique use of mirrors and portals coupled with dreams reshapes this mystery into a genre-blending fusion of fantasy, thriller, and mystical allure. She delivers a cast that is both inquisitive and knowledgeable, capably intertwining the metaphysical with reality." – The BookLife Prize

"This captivating story beautifully illustrates how nature, the elements, dreams, and human connection serve as guides, revealing the profound interplay between our physical reality and the unseen dimensions of mind, spirit, and emotion. It reminds us that nothing is working against us—everything conspires to help us grow, evolve, and embrace life's mysteries. Through an intricately woven narrative, the author explores the next frontier of multidimensional living. A visionary and uplifting read that inspires us to see beyond the ordinary and step into the expansive possibilities of existence of the unseen world. This story serves as a reminder that we are spiritual beings have a temporary human experience on earth and that when we only use our five senses, we can get stuck in the illusion of being just physical. The author further encourages us to deepen our awareness and step into our true power by embracing our spiritual and psychic gifts and stepping into who we truly are as multidimensional beings." – Cathleen Beerkens, Bestselling Author of *Your Creator Matrix*

"Lose yourself in the ancestral mansion of Maple Hollow where haunted mirrors line the walls and dreams guide the way. Rich with sorcerer-themed imagery, everyday witches, and secret portals, this atmospheric tale combines edge-of-the seat action with metaphysical musings on the self and the soul." – Katherine Bell, PhD, *The Dream Journal Podcast*

"A mystical tale which unfolds through dream imagery and includes wisdom to discover who you truly are. A magical story of good vs evil which includes wisdom on how to access your inner strength and power." – Meera Ishaya, Author of *Surrender is good for the Soul: The art of surrendering to gain fulfilment in life*

"I felt the magic of this world from the very first chapter. The imagery is captivating and so easy to visualize, and the characters are likeable right away. Megan's love for Hannah and Maple Hollow is clear from each enchanting word." – Kirsten McNeill, *Worthy Writers Coaching*

THE DREAM MIRRORS

A METAPHYSICAL MYSTERY OF MAGICK

MEGAN MARY

INNER REALMS PUBLISHING

For more information contact:
Inner Realms Publishing info@innerrealmspublishing.com

MeganMary.com

Book cover by Dragana Nikolic

Illustration by Melissa Rankin

Editing by Ivywild Editing & Writing Services LLC and Edit Experts

979-8-9900882-6-9 (hardcover)

979-8-9900882-9-0 (dustjacket)

979-8-9900882-5-2 (paperback)

979-8-9900882-8-3 (ebook)

Library of Congress Control Number: 2025907099

To my husband, whose heroic efforts saved our home and cats Merlin & Milu, from what could have been a devastating and tragic fire in the winter of 2025. It is only through his quick thinking and courageous action, the protection of our spirit guides, and the synchronistic alignment of all planets on that day, that this book is now in your hands.

CONTENTS

FOREWORD

Readers of Megan Mary's previous book, *The Dream Haunters*, will be pleased to follow the adventures of her characters in her latest book, *The Dream Mirrors: A Metaphysical Mirror of Magick*. The narrative pitches the reader into a world of dreams, storms, mirrors, cats, pumpkins, and spells. I say "pitched" because at the heart of the narrative is the vortex, the sense of matter in circular motion, whether as minute as an atom or as vast as a galaxy. The author weaves dream interpretation seamlessly into the series of events. At every turn, I recognised the interpretation methodologies as laid out in my book, *Dreams: Exploring Uncharted Depths of Consciousness* (Mandrake, 2020). The story's setting, Skye Manor, is on an island remote, yet connected to the cosmos. Nor does the author shun technology, the characters (Hannah, Aunt Jewelia, Morgan, Ashlin, Old Man Adams) making a healthy use of cars and telephones as they battle the dark forces of the Illusionix. And dispelling illusion is central to the tale, as Hannah is presented with the philosophy of the mirror, learning that what she (and we) see in the glass is but one step towards finding the true self.

The mirror is a topic that I explore in my later book, *Wicked Uncles and Haunted Cellars: What the Gothic Heroine Tells Us Today* (Greenwich Exchange, 2024). Other gothic motifs that endear Megan Mary's narrative to me include the ever-pervading storm, the old house and family connections, and unravelling mysterious documents. I was touched also with her selective use of the Celtic language, actually Irish, which I learned while growing up in Dublin. Above all is the warm sense of connection between the female characters, the sense that all women (fictional and real) can throw off victimhood and take our own steps towards self-actualisation, that we are not helpless pawns. This is a message I stress again and again in "*Wicked Uncles*", the gothic heroine being an intelligent, energetic, and rational trope emergent in the literature of the time. Since "The Dream Mirrors" is the second in Megan Mary's series, the time to get acquainted with her fiction is now.

- Mary Phelan, Author of *Dreams: Exploring Uncharted Depths of Consciousness* and *Wicked Uncles and Haunted Cellars: What the Gothic Heroine Tells Us Today*

PROLOGUE

9:36PM SEPTEMBER 9, 2009

Rain pummeled the hood of her cloak as Hannah ran fast into the woods. The sky cracked open with an earth-shattering clap of thunder, and multiple bolts of lightning activated across the vastness above Skye Manor. Her feet fell heavily upon the moist soil, her heart racing in her chest. The metal clanged on the lantern she held as it thrashed rapidly to and fro. Tree branches seemed to be trying to block her path as she sought a way through the thick woods.

Ahead of her, another cloaked figure ran at full speed. The woman ducked and held her arms up against the branches, swinging wildly in defense.

"Wait! Wait!" Hannah yelled, desperation welling up inside her. The storm's deafening thunder rocking her core each time it released another onslaught; it felt as if she were on a battlefield of darkness. The trees that had seemed so welcoming during the day had now become obstacles preventing her desperate attempts to move through them.

At that moment the figure began to slow her pace and stagger from side to side. Hannah closed in, extending her hand outward, the tips of her fingers just touching the cloak as it fell. She attempted to catch it but the dead weight of the woman inside crashed to the ground into a soggy pile of leaves. Hannah swooped down to kneel over her, grasping her by the shoulders and shaking her. "Jezebelle! Jezebelle!" she said urgently, but there was no response. Jezebelle lay solidly still, unconscious, frozen.

CHAPTER ONE

THE FOG

3:33 AM SEPTEMBER 9, 2009

Earlier, that very morning, while everyone was sleeping in the manor and the moon was still high in the sky, the mysterious fog of the island of Maple Hollow began to rise off the sea and creep slow and low onto the manor grounds. Having left its watery rest, it crawled onto the rocks near the shore, penetrating every nook and cranny. Once it had filled the empty spaces, it began rolling over the tops of them like a gentle wave. It crept into the vast pumpkin patch around the manor, wetting the elaborate vines and coating the large gourds with a dewy mist. It moved past the first strands of grass onto the long walkway that led from the sea to the manor, filling the space between the towering shrubs that lined the pathway. Further it spread, not dissipating but rather gaining speed as it made its way from sea to shingle.

As it approached the manor it rose higher, turning into a towering tornado that rose up and up until it reached the open window of Hannah's bedroom, high above the ground. Hannah was fast asleep in her bed, the gentle purr of Midnight the black cat vibrating near her head on her pillow. The fog crept into the window, first as wispy fingers, then undulating and rising into fullness as it filled the entire bottom of the room from floor to bed.

Midnight raised his head, noticing the change in moisture and temperature in the room. His eyes grew wide as he perused the fog surrounding them, his whiskers twitching and ears rotating from side to side. He rose from his slumber and stood shifting his weight, one of his front paws on Hannah's chest. He slowly exhaled on Hannah's face, his whiskers gently tickled her nose.

Hannah began to awaken. She moved her fingers. Then, in an instant, her eyes snapped open, as if she instinctively sensed someone was in the room. Also at that moment, as if there were a vacuum in another dimension sucking it all up, the fog instantly poured into the mirror over the dresser across the room from the bed, and it was gone.

Hannah sat up, unaware of what had just crossed her path. She gave a few gentle pets to Midnight's head and back and looked over at the slightly open window. Behind her, a swirl of fog circled in the mirror, the final remnants of its passage to the other side.

Undetected until its time of recognition. Lying in wait for that moment of reflection to come.

CHAPTER TWO

THE PARTY

6:33PM SEPTEMBER 9, 2009

A great storm surged outside the warm and dry confines of Skye Manor. The rain beat against the tall, arch-shaped windows that lined one wall of the great hall, the panes gilded with wrought-iron bars. On either side of the windows, heavy velvet curtains hung. The lights were dim. In the middle, stood a stately dining table, large enough to fit twenty or more people. It had been the great gathering place of old. So many important meetings this hall had seen ... if only the table could whisper the tales.

The gentle sound of distant, lovely piano music filled the room. From the rafters of the hall hung a long row of ornate chandeliers, their metal curving onto itself in a round pumpkin shape. Tiny tassels and crystals hung from each one, catching the flames and making them dance around the room.

A hearty fire churned and cracked inside the grand fireplace, its bright light reflected on the stone floor. Above it hung a large mirror, its glass as dark as a black hole in a galaxy. Candlelight flickered as wax slowly dripped down the sides of the multiple candles that were balanced in large iron candelabras on the enormous table. Ancient columns of cream stone, cracked from years of aging, rose up from the ground towards the sky.

Large decanters of wine and delicate champagne flutes were placed carefully around the table, circling the baroque tapestry runner gilded with etchings of Celtic knotwork. Strewn about every corner of the great hall were large portraits of people legacies old, their faces telling a tale all their own. They sat silent as the room awaited its guests.

The table was set for six, three on each side. It was spilling with fruits, nuts, and breads all piled upon opulent serving trays. Halves of oranges, crisp apples, persimmons, and pomegranates were nestled among opulent black, red, and green grapes. Hazelnuts, walnuts, almonds, cashews, and nuts of all shapes and sizes filled in the empty spaces until there wasn't a speck of space left.

The sound of clicking heels echoed through the room as Jewelia Skye descended the stairs. Her slender frame was wrapped in a cascading sumptuous velvet dress. Her long black hair tumbled past her shoulders as she crossed the foyer, entered the great hall, and surveyed the scene to make sure everything was prepared. The guests would be arriving any minute to join herself and her niece Hannah, and she wanted it to be perfect.

Her concentration was broken by a cracking knock at the front door, caused by the manor's heavy iron gargoyle knocker. She glided into the foyer and opened the door with anticipation. "Morgan!" she said, a rich smile crossing her deep red lips. She reached out her hand to welcome her in. "You're just in time."

"Well, hello, my dear," Madame Morgan said warmly, lowering the hood of her cloak as she crossed the threshold, revealing her long silver curls and deep green eyes.

"Come inside and warm your bones." Jewelia ushered her longtime friend toward the parlor that opened off the foyer. It was filled with lavish violet upholstered furnishings and featured a large window flanked on either side by tall white columns and red curtains.

At that moment, Old Man Adams appeared from down the hall carrying a large tray of wine glasses filled to the brim with glowing liquid. He had been the caretaker of Skye Manor since Jewelia was young. Living in his own cottage tucked away in a cozy corner of the grounds, he would happily offer his assistance to Hannah and Jewelia whenever special occasions arose. He shined up his usual weathered appearance for the dinner by donning a crisp white collared shirt, satin black vest, and a dark cap to obscure his snowy white hair. "Can I offer you a drink?" Jewelia asked Morgan.

"Yes, yes," her friend replied enthusiastically, reaching for a glass from the tray. "Thank you, my dear," she said to Old Man Adams with a smile.

"My lady," he said, extending a warm welcome bow and nod in return.

"Good evening, Morgan," Hannah said from behind the grand piano. Her fingers still gently twinkled across the keys, filling the parlor with delightful ambient music. The train of her long dress sashayed across the bench as she moved.

"Hannah, my dear, you look lovely," Morgan said as she approached the piano. Their eyes locked in a meaningful gaze. Hannah smiled, feeling her heart warming inside. It was always validating to receive genuine compliments. It made her feel more confident and assured.

Another knock at the front door broke the silence. Old Man Adams turned and slowly walked toward the door, letting in the guest and taking her wrap.

"Ashlin!" Hannah exclaimed, looking up from the keys.

"Hannah," Ashlin Aldona said moments later in excitement as she entered the parlor. She was a bit older than Hannah, but not by too much. She worked at the local library in Maple Hollow. Old Man Adams had once told Hannah that Ashlin was the keeper of all the island's wisdom.

"So glad you could make it," Hannah said while admiring Ashlin's outfit. Her skin glowed in the reflection from her golden gown which warmed her complexion. Mahogany curls fell loosely around her face and nestled around the tortoise-shell glasses perched upon her freckled dainty nose as she took a seat in a stately antique chair next to the piano.

"Jewelia, Morgan," Ashlin said with a smile as Adams offered her a glass of wine. Light conversations filled the room with laughter and whispers, as hors d'oeuvres were passed skillfully on glistening gilded trays by Wendy, an old friend of Jewelia's who had moved out west. Because Wendy was a chef extraordinaire, Jewelia had offered to compensate her to not only join, but prepare, their very special meal. While observing her carefully coiffed red hair, Hannah noticed the gentle kindness in the way Wendy carried herself. She seemed to exude a friendly nature that put everyone around her immediately at ease.

"I'm so glad to see this in person," another guest said as she entered the parlor, fluttering her eyelashes and scanning every inch of the room.

"It's marvelous, isn't it?" Ashlin replied, peering over her glasses with a hint of pride.

Hannah looked up from the piano to see the new arrival. It was Jezebelle, who she'd been told was a friend of Wendy's. At first glance the young woman looked like the epitome of beauty, or at least according to what society defines as beauty. It almost made Hannah feel a tad inadequate. Jezebelle's hair was perfect, blonde and shiny. Her makeup, while overdone, made her skin glow; her dress was tightly wrapped around her shapely body, with a low V-shaped neckline. Hannah immediately felt dissatisfied with the dress she had chosen. While she loved the color, which was a deep purple, the girlish frilly ruffles, A-line waist, and long sleeves made her feel like she was swimming in a giant frock when compared against Jezebelle's tight dress. She suddenly wished she'd worn something else.

Jezebelle had offered to join Wendy in her hometown of Maple Hollow. They both lived out west, and Jezebelle had told Wendy she was keen to explore New England and the manor Wendy talked about so much. Jezebelle's obsession with beauty was obvious. But the more Hannah looked at her, the more she could see that Jezebelle was trying to hide something. Her lips were overly plump, like they had reacted to an ingested toxin, and that wasn't the only thing. From front to back, every womanly aspect of Jezebelle seemed to have had a little help, apparently surgical or cosmetic. There was little that was natural about her body. Even her skin had a summerish hue not obtained in chill

September air. Hannah tried to set aside her uncomfortable feelings to focus on her music.

"Look at these paintings," Jezebelle gawked as her fingers ran along the gilded edges of the large frames gracing the ancestral paintings hanging on the walls.

"I wonder what's for dinner?" Ashlin asked. Hannah thought she could hear her stomach grumble.

"Wendy has planned a spectacular feast," Jewelia reassured everyone. "Dinner will be served at eight o'clock." She smiled. "Relax and enjoy the music!" She gestured to Hannah, giving her center stage.

The conversation drifted as Old Man Adams again offered each of the women a drink. For a short while, the group sat silently, listening to Hannah's piano playing, observing the room and each other.

Eventually, the large grandfather clock struck eight and Jewelia rose from her chair. "Ladies, let us all take our seats at the table."

They followed Jewelia across the foyer into the great hall, approached the large table and looked for their name tags. Torches lined the stone walls, each with its own sparkling flame letting off a mysterious orange glow. There were six place settings, each for a very special guest.

Jewelia stood at the far end of the table, an ornate pipe organ behind her, as each woman took her seat. Hannah took her place in the middle of one side, next to what would be her aunt's seat. Madame Morgan sat down across from Jewelia's chair, nearest the large fireplace. On Hannah's other side, Ashlin took her place. Jezebelle searched for her place setting and took her seat at the far end, across from Ashlin, leaving the seat in between herself and Morgan for Wendy.

Jewelia began to speak. "Thank you all for being here tonight. It is my and Hannah's pleasure to host you here at Skye Manor. Let us dine and celebrate. Please enjoy the feast," she said, holding her wine glass in the air to prompt the others. The guests clapped, smiled, and nodded as they each raised their glass in toast. Old Man Adams carefully delivered the first course of pumpkin soup, presented in small carved out pumpkins. He smiled with a twinkle in his eye as he served them one by one to the guests.

"Feast on the pumpkins from our patch, my loves. They will fortify you," Jewelia said.

The first course was followed by a series of scrumptious additional courses, hand-delivered to each and every woman by Old Man Adams. They dined and conversed for nearly an hour. The gentle sounds of the fireplace crackled in the quiet moments as everyone indulged their senses.

"Wendy, you are a culinary genius," Jewelia said as she licked her lips savoring the flavors.

"Indeed, it's quite miraculous. You have exquisite taste as always, Jewelia," Morgan agreed full-heartedly.

As the second and third courses were served, amongst the clanking of the cutlery and dishes, small conversations popped up between the guests.

"Do I detect truffle?" Ashlin asked.

"Of course," Jewelia replied. "Wendy curates only the best from the island when she's in town. Her gourmet skills are truly her magick. I wouldn't trust anyone else in my kitchen."

Hannah found this endorsement comforting, as both she and Jewelia had suffered food poisoning from one of the local cafés a few years back. Of course, that had actually involved much more nefarious circumstances.

But ever since then, she wasn't taking any chances with who cooked her meals, and neither was Jewelia.

"I don't usually get to eat like this," Jezebelle observed in delight. Hannah suspected that Jezebelle's worldly experience was fairly limited. She didn't seem to have the same sophistication as the other guests, nor was she privy to the formality of four-course meals. She peered across the table at her. "And what is it that you do, Jezebelle?"

"I work at a beauty parlor," Jezebelle replied, flipping her hair.

Hannah was not surprised. She got the sense, at least from Jezebelle's appearance, that she was primarily concerned with just that.

"Enjoy, my dears," Morgan said, smiling at them both in her wise way.

Jezebelle observed quietly as Ashlin and Hannah exchanged smiles.

"That organ is amazing," Jezebelle remarked after a bit. "Do you often play it?"

"Yes," Hannah and Jewelia answered, nearly at the same time. Then smiled at each other. "Yes, we both do," Jewelia finished.

"I've always found music to be the ethereal avenue to our souls," Morgan observed.

Eventually, dessert was served: pumpkin coffeecake sprinkled with dash of cinnamon, nutmeg, and all-spice, and topped off with a dollop of whipped cream. When they had all finished eating, Jewelia stood at the head of the table, clinking her spoon upon her glass to break the din.

CHAPTER THREE

THE PORTAL

"Attention ladies! I hope you all enjoyed your meal. Tonight, as you know, we are gathered here at Skye Manor for a momentous occasion. On this night, there is a great portal opening: the portal of the 999. There are six of us gathered here, as six is the mirror reflection of nine. You may or may not know the lore and the power of this portal. The ninth day of the ninth month presents a cosmic opportunity to release what no longer serves you and align your spiritual essence. You're all gathered here tonight as an invitation to harness it," she said, raising her glass in a toast.

As she spoke, a purple galaxy appeared above their heads and began to swirl in the vast ceiling.

"Now that your dinner plates have been cleared, you will find before you yet another setting. But this course will be quite different."

Old Man Adams made his way around the table, gathering dishes. What remained in front of each woman was an ornate silver charger in the shape of a mirror with black glass. They had previously been hidden below all of the other plates, but now that those were cleared, the chargers were all that remained.

"I invite you now to grasp the charger and hold it up in front of you. What you see before you, my friends, is a mirror. Your gateway into the 999 portal. What you find there is unique to you. This process is not for the faint of heart, and some of you may not like what you see. But I trust you will all find the answers you seek in the end."

Jezebelle lifted her mirror immediately, checking her reflection. She obviously had been wanting to check it since she arrived at the manor and was more than happy to gaze upon it now.

Morgan and Hannah lifted theirs without hesitation. Then Ashlin followed suit.

The lights began to dim, and each mirror darkened until they were all black as night. A stillness fell upon the room; only the flames dancing in the hearth continued to move. Time passed slowly as each guest stared into her mirror. The purple galaxy in the ceiling began to swirl like stars in the sky, creating its own canopy.

"Let the magick of Skye Manor be your guide on your journey," Jewelia intoned.

It seemed clear that Jezebelle, practicing smiles at her reflection, was content to just admire herself. "Try to look beyond your reflection," Morgan offered. "There is so much more to discover."

But Jezebelle didn't see the point in that. She touched her fingers to her hair and face, primping herself. Ashlin, however, seemed to be lost in a trance, sitting in a silent stupor as she stared. A wry smile crossed Wendy's face as it appeared her visions were beginning to develop.

Suddenly, an iridescent owl radiating an ethereal glow appeared above the gathering, but it was no normal owl. It flew in through an open window at one end of the great hall and out an open window at the other. Hannah's eyes followed its path, and as she gazed out the tall windows, she saw trails of bright stars shooting across the sky behind the owl. Then a strong wind blew through the hall, extinguishing the candles and the flames of the fire, shrouding everyone in darkness.

Jewelia and Morgan stood quickly, matches in hand, and went about relighting the torches on the walls.

"Very well now, my friends. The owl has made its appearance," Jewelia said. "Now we can proceed."

But right then, a woman's gasp filled the air. "Where's Jezebelle?" Wendy asked. "She was sitting right here a second ago..." There was a look of disbelief on her face.

"Perhaps she just went to the bathroom. Would you care to check, my love?" Jewelia motioned to Hannah and she rose from her chair. Everyone remained still, as if too much motion might disturb the moment.

"She's not there," Hannah said when she returned from down the hall.

"Well, she must be around here somewhere. She was sitting right next to me and the lights only went out for a second," Wendy insisted, positive that her friend couldn't have moved that fast.

"Things are not always as they appear," Morgan murmured, in her usual mysterious yet revealing way.

"Did you see Jezebelle run out?" Ashlin asked Old Man Adams, who was standing dumbfounded with the tray in his hand.

"Why no, I'm sorry, little lady. I didn't see anything."

"Ok, let's not panic," Jewelia said. "I'm sure she's somewhere in the manor. Let's break up and go look for her. She can't be far."

Hannah and Morgan headed toward the back of the manor. As they walked down the long hallway, purple flashes illuminated the walls from the lightning outside. Hannah placed one hand on the back doorknob, and with her other hand, grabbed cloaks from the row of hooks that stood waiting by the door. She passed one to Morgan, who had retrieved two large lanterns.

"Matches?" Morgan asked searchingly.

"Yes, got them." Hannah flipped the lid on a small metal container attached to the wall near a bench, a cozy place to sit when coming inside from the rain to remove wet outerwear. "We may want these, too," she added, grabbing two strings from the hooks; from each one hung a small whistle. She had always wondered why there were whistles in such a peculiar place, but now she knew why.

Striking a match swiftly on the metal container, Hannah lit each lantern and the women stepped out into the rain, cloaks obscuring their heads. They each extended their lantern to illuminate the ground before them. The storm was swirling around them, catching the bottoms of their cloaks and thrashing the material to and fro around their ankles. They ran down the long cypress-lined pathway and through the pumpkin patch in the hard driving rain, toward the protection of the forest, their feet becoming wet as they sunk into the moist soil. Once under the thick canopy of the trees, the rain didn't fall as hard and they could look up a bit more easily to watch where they were going.

A long, rolling thunder cracked across the sky, dragging on into the indefinite horizon far beyond the island. The winds whipped the sea that crashed into the rocks on the shore, but they were deep within the forest now, nestled within the depth of the murky, dark trees.

"Jezebelle!" Hannah shouted, echoed by Morgan,

"Jezebelle, are you out here?" Morgan yelled over the storm. "Watch the trees for signs," she said to Hannah. "They'll lead you back to the manor should you lose your way."

Although Hannah had heard her, she realized she wasn't quite sure what Morgan meant by signs. Did she mean actual signs attached to the trees, or something more obscure? Knowing her, it was likely the latter. But Hannah knew they didn't have time to discuss that right now.

As they approached a fork in the path, Hannah motioned to Morgan that she was going to venture off to the left. Morgan nodded and turned off to the right. Each woman walked slowly and carefully, their feet crunching the fallen leaves beneath them, now becoming soggy from the relentless rain.

"Jezebelle!" Hannah yelled over and over as she slowly waved her lantern, casting a circular light around herself and into different parts of the forest. As she descended into the trees, she felt the passage of time slow the more she realized how cavernous and isolated the forest was. It was as if its darkness were enveloping her.

Suddenly Hannah saw movement. She began to follow, first with a quickened step, then at a faster pace, and then she found herself running. There was someone else in the forest with them. She couldn't see the person's face because it was obscured by the dark hood of a cloak. She chased after the shadowy figure. "Jezebelle, is that you?" But no sooner had she come within reach of the figure than it collapsed on the ground in a large pile of leaves out of her reach.

Hannah reached for the whistle around her neck and placed it to her mouth as she leaned in for a closer look. Taking a deep breath, she blew all the air she could muster, like a traffic guard announcing it was time to cross the road. As her hands cleared away the leaves, her anticipation and anxiety rose at what she might be revealing.

She felt her eyes widen. It was Jezebelle. She dropped the whistle from her mouth.

"Jezebelle? Jezebelle?" She sprang into action and shook Jezebelle's arm vigorously, but there was no response. Hannah blew into her whistle firmly now, to be sure Morgan would hear. It seemed forever, but she finally heard the sound of feet crashing through the leaves and the clanking of Morgan's lantern coming closer. She continued, guiding Morgan through the woody darkness with the shrill sound, as she desperately wiped away the layer of leaves obscuring her view.

"Hannah, did you find something?" Morgan came bounding through the woods, branches crashing around her. "Oh, my dears," she said as she approached, finding Hannah holding Jezebelle in her arms on the ground.

Chapter Four

THE ICEHOUSE

"Let's get her out of the rain," Morgan said as she stood over Jezebelle's feet, motioning to Hannah to pick up her shoulders. "It's only a few steps to the icehouse. We can bring her there."

Hannah wasn't sure what Morgan was talking about, but she wanted to get out of the rain just the same. She grabbed Jezebelle's shoulders and as she did, the hood of her cloak dropped off her head. The moon gleamed through the trees and reflected on her face. Hannah could see Jezebelle had been crying, and imprinted on her face was a terrified look that gave Hannah pause. Her eyes were wide open, gazing in a deathly stare.

Morgan, walking backwards but knowing exactly where she was going, led the way to a small hill. Hannah would not have even noticed it, but within the earth was a small door. Morgan uttered an incantation under her breath, and the door slowly began to open.

"Let's put her in here for now. She'll be safe from the storm," she said as they brought Jezebelle in and set her body down on a small cot that stood against the back wall. The structure was domed with dark gray brick-lined walls.

"What is this place? I've never seen it before," said Hannah. She had been exploring the grounds of her family's manor for almost two years now and somehow never discovered this.

"It's an old icehouse," Morgan replied. "Back in the day, castles always had one, small rooms built into the earth as a place to keep the ice cold. A natural freezer, it is. Your family continued that legacy," she explained as Hannah, shivering, attempted to wrap her cloak closer around her.

Morgan turned to Jezebelle. "Can you hear me?" she said, attempting to check her pulse, tapping her hands, and speaking loudly over the rain. But Jezebelle didn't respond. She appeared frozen, as if she was in a coma, but somehow her eyes were still open.

"Jezebelle, wake up," Hannah said as she too attempted to rouse her from her strange sleep. But neither of them could awaken her.

"What happened to her?" Hannah asked Morgan, the wind blowing hard on the door and the thunder continuing to boom above them.

Morgan didn't answer. "Run back to the manor, get Jewelia, and go to the grimoire," she instructed.

"But what about you? Are you sure?" Hannah asked.

"I'll be fine, dear, I'll watch over her. Run now!" Morgan said.

Without further protest, Hannah ran out into the storm and headed back to the manor. By the time she reached the back door, her cloak was soaked, the ends of her hair wet and sticking to her face. She walked down the long hallway that connected the back of the house with the foyer and then back into the great hall.

"We found her! She's with Morgan at the icehouse," Hannah announced. A collective sigh of relief came from the room. Whispers were exchanged, some in criticism of Jezebelle, some in sympathy.

"But...Morgan sent me to get you," she said to Jewelia. "She needs your help." She tried to not reveal Jezebelle's state. Pulling Jewelia aside by the elbow, she dragged her into the foyer. "Jezebelle is in some kind of coma, she's unresponsive. Morgan said to go to the grimoire."

"Coma? The grimoire?!" Jewelia raised one eyebrow. "What is going on?" She asked rhetorically, already starting to suspect the worst. "Come, my dear."

Her long velvet evening gown sashayed along the ground, the ends of Hannah's wet dress sloshing along behind her like a dark swamp creature crawling out of the depths. Jewelia pushed on the small, unnoticeable door under the stairs, creaking loudly as it opened inward.

CHAPTER FIVE

THE LIBRARY

They both stepped into the darkness and proceeded down the short hallway that turned toward the library. As they entered the large room, Jewelia approached the mantel above the fireplace and reached for a vase filled with long matches. Next to it was a large metal lantern. She fumbled for a match, striking it against the metal exterior of the lantern and then passing it inside to activate the flame.

As Hannah's eyes traced the lantern light illuminating the floor-to-ceiling bookshelves, she felt nostalgia for the long days she had spent with Aunt Jewelia in the library over the past few years. It contained so many books that had shed light on the secrets of Maple Hollow, teaching her of its energetic properties, ley lines, and vortexes. The more Hannah learned, the more she felt tied to the island. Her ancient lineage was expanding its roots, grounding her in her family's legacy. Its magick and secrets had become part of her consciousness, her future.

Hannah's dress snagged on an uneven floor board. It was the one that led to the secret room she had discovered soon after arriving at Skye Manor. Now she bent over to release the snagged piece of cloth and reached for the handle to the trapdoor that was obscured within the wood. It was unassuming to a passerby, but noticeable to someone with the knowledge of its existence.

Her eyes looked up at Jewelia, who nodded silently and passed her the lantern. Hannah grasped the handle and pulled the square floorboard toward her, opening up the passageway.

They descended into the dark opening, Hannah going first, holding the lantern up by her eyes as if the light would activate a vision into the unseen, into the darkness they were about to be enveloped by.

The staircase was spiral and tenuous. She pulled up her skirt as she carefully placed each foot on the stairs, hoping to not trip herself. Jewelia followed closely behind her, her left hand sliding across the carvings on the stairwell walls. When they reached the bottom, they met with a large wall of books. Hannah held the lantern next to the bookstacks and Jewelia reached out to tug on a large volume adorned with Celtic knotwork down the spine. The book tipped toward her and a bookshelf door began to give way, creaking loudly as it slowly opened.

They entered the room and approached the lectern, on top of which was a large ancient book. It was the *Grimoire de Skye*, the family book of shadows Hannah had discovered when she was solving the mystery of her aunt's disappearance. It was how she had learned about the power of the pumpkin patch. But this book held so many more secrets. It contained hundreds of years of wisdom that she couldn't possibly absorb in just a few years. But she and Jewelia had hope in their hearts that the book would reveal what they needed to know at this moment...that it would assist them in saving Jezebelle, whatever had happened to her.

Hannah had observed the book move on its own before, seemingly flopping open to a particular section, the weight of the hard cover giving way and the light pages flipping to an opportune spot, seemingly inviting the reader to peruse that teaching. But on this night, that did not happen. The book stayed shut and still.

Jewelia raised her hands, holding them above the grimoire and closing her eyes. She began to chant an incantation, a request. After a few moments, she opened her eyes and glanced over at Hannah.

"It's not working?" Hannah asked finally.

"I'm asking for guidance from our elders, but it sounds like this is something beyond what we've encountered before. Perhaps the guidance is not already written, and we are being asked to discover it."

"I thought the grimoire contained all the information we would need to do the work our family is called to do," Hannah said, confused at her assumption.

"That's not wrong, usually," Jewelia said, hesitating. "But it is Mercury retrograde right now and as such, I have a strong sense that there is something different this time. Perhaps you should try it." She stepped aside and let Hannah stand in front of the lectern. "Ask it in your mind for the truth to be revealed."

Hannah stood in front of the thick volume, raised her hands over it, and closed her eyes. She asked in her mind for an answer. The cover of the book started to quiver, as if it was deciding, with hesitation, that it might have to oblige the request.

"There," Jewelia said, her eyes darting at the cover as she saw it begin to move. "Keep going, dear."

As Hannah gained more assurance, she focused her energy even more sharply on the book. This time, the cover flopped open and the pages began to flip. She opened her eyes at the sound of the cover hitting the lectern. Then the book came to a halt and lay still. Hannah looked at it. "Page 999," she noted.

Jewelia's eyes became wide. "The 999 portal. Yes, of course, something has come through the portal and caused these misfortunes. The question is, what. Whatever came through is what we are up against. It is what has caused Jezebelle's demise, her terrible state. But what is it?"

They both leaned in for a closer look. On the page was an illustration of a large, ornate mirror. Coming out of it was what could only be described as a dark, demonic figure. Below the illustration was a caption that Hannah read aloud: "*Illusionix, An Ceann Dorcha Den Fantasm.* What does that mean?"

"It means, the Dark One of Phantasm. Illusionix is a trickster spirit."

"It says here that the doorway to Phantasm can only be opened on a day of celestial alignment. Is this what got to Jezebelle?" Hannah asked, turning to Jewelia with concern.

"I'm not sure, but it is up to us to find out. Come, let's go see Morgan."

Jewelia and Hannah went back up the spiral steps to the library and then out the small door under the stairs. Wendy and Ashlin were in the parlor picking up empty glasses from the pre-dinner gathering and placing them on trays.

"Did you find anything?" Wendy rushed up to Jewelia and Hannah.

"We checked the grimoire," Jewelia said. "It's the Dark One of Phantasm, the Illusionix. Have you heard of it?"

Wendy shook her head.

"I might have, but I'll have to research it further," Ashlin offered.

"What if it's coming for us?" Hannah asked impatiently.

"Gathering whatever information we can, as quickly as possible, will help Jezebelle," Jewelia replied, looking concerned but resolved.

Ashlin passed her gaze from Jewelia to Hannah. "I'll run to the library right now and see what I can find," she said gently, pushing her glasses back up to the bridge of her nose.

"Thank you, love," Jewelia said. "Hannah, run back to Morgan and let her know what we found."

Hannah nodded and the four women parted ways. Hannah began to run, her heart pounding in her chest.

CHAPTER SIX

THE DISAPPEARANCE

Hannah sped down the dark hallway, away from the warmth of the parlor. She placed her hand on the knob to the back door, pushing it open more forcefully now. She ran out into the storm, through the forest, and toward the icehouse. On the way there, she ran into Old Man Adams coming back from searching the grounds.

"We found Jezebelle, she's not well," Hannah explained.

"But where's Jewelia? What did she say?" he asked Hannah.

"We checked the grimoire. It's something called Illusionix. Jewelia sent Ashlin to the town library. She said we need to gather all the information we can to help Jezebelle."

"You know I'll do anything I can to help." He put his hand on Hannah's shoulder.

"Thanks. I'm going to go check on Jezebelle and Morgan."

But rather than run right back to the icehouse, Hannah had another idea to try first. She ran to the pumpkin patch and yanked one of the pumpkins from the vine. She then found shelter in a small shed near the edge of the forest line and placed the pumpkin before her. Setting her hands on it, she became still and went within her mind, to a place beyond the building she occupied. Her breath led her through a labyrinth. But in that place, as she waited, she did not see Jezebelle.

She had been perfecting this method over the past two years as she worked with her aunt to free people from the Dream Haunters, evil energies that trapped people within their dreams. However, she was not picking up on what Jezebelle was feeling, and she could not detect whether she might be trapped or if she could free her. Frustrated, she opened her eyes and abruptly stopped. *Why was this not working?* It had worked before for her, without her even trying. *What was different this time?*

But there wasn't time to spare. Hannah was out of breath by the time she reached the icehouse. The rain had let up a bit, but the lightning was still strong and fast. Thoughts raced through her mind. She wondered who the Illusionix was, as she'd certainly never heard of such a thing. Jewelia had mentioned their family line had battled dark forces many years ago. Were there even more she didn't know about? She began to get that familiar feeling of anxiety in her chest.

She had successfully helped rescue her aunt from captivity by the Dream Haunters, and she had discovered so much about herself in the two years since she came to Maple Hollow. But this? Hannah suddenly felt completely unprepared, scared even, and began to doubt any ability she had come to know as her own. She pulled the hood of her cloak closer to her face, protecting it from the harsh and unpredictable wind. When she burst through the rickety door of the icehouse, her eyes immediately flew to Jezebelle, still lying on the cot. But Morgan was not with her.

"Morgan? Morgan, I'm back," she announced, assuming maybe Morgan had retreated to a dark corner in search of a remedy for Jezebelle. But there was no reply.

"Morgan?" Hannah said once more, a bit quieter and with a bit more dismay. She walked around the room, looking for clues, evidence of what Morgan might have been doing while she was back at the manor. But she was nowhere to be found.

Why would she leave Jezebelle? It certainly wasn't in Morgan's nature to abandon someone in need, much less someone unconscious. Perhaps there was a secret tunnel? Or maybe she had sought out additional help and was out in the storm somewhere seeking out a solution they hadn't thought of.

Hannah opened the door, the rain dripping from the frame onto her cloak.

"Morgan!" she yelled out the door into the darkness. But there was no reply.

Fear struck in her chest. She didn't know much about the dark forces that had taken hold of Jezebelle, but she did know a thing or two about the Dream Haunters. They had trapped Jewelia in her nightmare. They had made her disappear. Now Morgan was gone, and all Hannah could think of was, *What if the Dream Haunters are back?*

Her mind raced as she tried to decide what to do. Should she also abandon Jezebelle, leaving her to fend for herself against who knows what, or stay here to watch over her while her good friend and confidant, whom she knew would not have left her, was gone.

She couldn't think straight. The faster her mind rolled, the more she tried to mull over her options, the more obscure her thoughts became. Jewelia was waiting for her back at the manor. Together they had to mobilize a plan against this new threat.

Hannah leaned over Jezebelle once more. She grasped her hand gently, then said, "Jezebelle, can you hear me? I'm not sure where Morgan went, but I have to go find her and get help. I promise I'll come back." She was vexed by her own words, the guilt beginning to ooze in her blood. How would she feel if someone just left her alone, lying unresponsive, in the icehouse?

But she had to put these thoughts out of her mind. She had to focus on the threat. She had to find Morgan. With Morgan gone, it would be up to herself, Ashlin, Wendy, and Jewelia to find out as much as they could about the Illusionix. They had no idea what they were up against.

She patted Jezebelle's hand a few times, then turned and ran back out into the woods. As she headed toward the manor, she continued to yell for Morgan, but there was no reply. Bursting back into the kitchen, Hannah first ran into Wendy.

"Did you see Morgan come back?" she first asked with hope.

"No, I'm sorry, I thought she was with you," Wendy replied, a confused look on her face as she stirred a small pot on the stove. "I'm making a compound for Jezebelle. It will at least lessen her anxiety."

"Good idea," Hannah said before she continued down the hallway back toward the foyer, where she met Old Man Adams again. "Have you seen Morgan?"

"No, why?" he asked.

"She was at the icehouse with Jezebelle, but she's not there now."

"Wendy would have seen her if she came through the back…" He paused pondering where else Morgan might be. "I'll go check my cabin. Maybe she went there."

Jewelia came out of the parlor to join them in the foyer. "What's happening?" she asked, stopping her stride, aware she was the only one who didn't know something.

"Morgan wasn't there…at the icehouse. I don't think she would have left Jezebelle there by herself," Hannah said.

"What? Well, where would she have gone?" Jewelia mused out loud as Old Man Adams darted away to go check his cabin.

"Maybe she ran back to Maple Moon to fetch a tincture. I'll call over there." Jewelia grabbed her phone. Morgan's metaphysical shop was one of the best places to find remedies to unusual ailments. Jewelia's tone seemed to imply there was no need to panic; perhaps Morgan had simply run for supplies.

But as she stood there listening to the phone ring on the other end, a look of deepening concern crossed her face. "There's no answer," she said, disconnecting the call. "But maybe she went to the greenhouse for a remedy?" She had a hopeful look in her eye. "I'll go check there." Before she departed, she placed her hand on Hannah's shoulder.

"Whatever this is, my love, and whatever we are about to face, remember you are the key. If something happens to me and we are separated again, you must hold that certainty inside you. Never lose it, and we will never lose each other."

Hannah reached for Jewelia's hand on her shoulder, giving Jewelia a quick, small smile of reassurance.

"You go to the icehouse. We'll go to the greenhouse. Hurry, we don't have much time," Jewelia said. She ran down the dark hallway and out the back door into the darkness.

CHAPTER SEVEN

THE REVERSAL

Hannah ran back to the icehouse to wait with Jezebelle. But soon enough Jewelia and Old Man Adams showed up and she knew by the distraught looks on their faces that they had not found Morgan or a remedy.

"Anything?" she asked, with a hopeful tone.

"No sign of her," Old Man Adams said with disappointment. "Let's get Jezebelle up to the manor. C'mon now." He motioned to Jewelia and Hannah to help.

Hannah and Jewelia each grasped a leg and Old Man Adams lifted under her shoulders. As they made their way back through the woods, the wind whipped around them and rain soaked their clothes. When they reached the back door to the kitchen, Wendy greeted them, opening the door.

"Oh my," Wendy said as she saw Jezebelle's state of paralysis and the frozen look of fear on her face. "There is something sinister about this that doesn't look right." She ushered them in.

They brought Jezebelle to the parlor and covered her from chest to feet with a warm blanket. "What happened to her?" Wendy asked urgently, rapidly blinking in disbelief and concern.

"That's what we'd all like to know," said Old Man Adams.

Hannah and Jewelia's eyes met with a look of determination. They both knew this event was yet another call for them to carry on their family legacy, which was to protect and guide others as Healers of the Hollow. They never knew when the call would arrive, or who it would be for. They were resolved once again to answer.

Hannah suddenly remembered the book on reversal magick she had discovered when Jewelia had disappeared. "Aunt Jewelia, can we reverse this? Whatever's happened to Morgan and Jezebelle, can we use reversal magick to undo it?"

"We certainly can try, love, although we must be careful. It is only to be used under extreme duress...which I guess this qualifies as. But there is much preparation to do."

Hannah and Jewelia ran to the library. As they entered, a large, shiny cat appeared behind them.

"Zoot!" Jewelia said with surprise. Hannah spun around to see who she was talking to. At the door stood a black cat, but it was not Midnight, nor any other cat Hannah had seen before.

"What?" Hannah said in confusion.

"It's Zooti! He is one of the cats of the manor. He only makes his appearance when the time is right. He is an elder of the wild cats that live in the forest. He must know we need his magick for this spell. Come now, he'll follow," she said.

Skye Manor really must have been made for cats, Hannah reflected as they made their way around the library to gather supplies. Every door had a small opening at the bottom carved into the shape of cat ears, ensuring free feline passage at all times; she knew Midnight appreciated this respectful gesture. She'd often watched him running rapidly through the openings in play, or slinking secretly through them to hide. And the manor contained so many windows to look out of, so many pillows and blankets for cats to rest on. So many corners to hide. There was no better place in the world for cats.

After collecting candles, incense, crystals, and other small symbolic trinkets, Hannah and Jewelia proceeded down the trap door and into the sanctum of the manor, carrying *The Art of Reversal Magick*. Once they reached it, Zooti immediately jumped up on the lectern and began rubbing his face on the book.

"See, he's telling us he's going to help," Jewelia said. "Quick, grab the cauldron."

Hannah retrieved a small cauldron of heavy iron. She placed it on the large table in the middle of the room. Jewelia proceeded to set a black candle on either side and one directly opposite from where they stood.

"Now light the incense," Jewelia said next. Hannah grabbed a long, black lighter and held it to the small stick. It sparked and a puff of smoke rose above them. The scent of amber and cinnamon filled the air.

Jewelia scribbled on two small pieces of parchment. Hannah could see the word "Illusionix," scrawled in black on one of them. She folded them and wrote "Morgan" on one and "Jezebelle" on the other.

"We'll need some basil and elderflower," Jewelia said. Hannah darted to the back wall, which was filled with shelves stacked with small bottles of herbs, stones, and powders. She scanned the shelves until she found the items, then brought the small vials to the table.

Jewelia inserted her fingertips in the vials, took a small pinch of each herb, and sprinkled them into the cauldron. "Mirror spirits causing trouble. Trapping Jezebelle in a bubble. Break her spell of paralyzed fear. Destroy the Illusionix who draws near," she intoned.

She then touched one of the parchments to the central candle, lighting it afire and dropped it into the cauldron.

Then she began to move her arms in a swirling pattern above the flames. "Lift the shadow. Free our sister. Pierce the darkness of this twister."

She lit the second parchment afire. Once the second process was completed, she stood in silence.

"It is done," she finally said. "Now there's a final step to do. We must spread the ashes to the wind, giving this to Mother Moon to finish."

She grabbed the cauldron and she and Hannah proceeded back up the stairs, into the library, down the hallway, and outside to the edge of the sea. "Ask for the wind to carry your intention to the moon," Jewelia said, passing the cauldron to Hannah.

Hannah wrapped her hands around the cast-iron pot. She stared up at the moon. She set her intention to heal Jezebelle and save Morgan, and then raised her arms. A strong gust of wind rose up, and Hannah tilted the pot just right so the wind picked up the ashes and carried them off in a swift cloud toward the sky.

"So mote it be," they both uttered in tandem. Then they both waited in silence for a moment.

"Let's go check on Jezebelle now," Jewelia said.

But as they entered the parlor where Jezebelle lay, they found her still unresponsive. Wendy, drawing on her culinary and potions prowess, had concocted a salve, which she had rubbed as a balm onto Jezebelle's cheeks. It had temporarily removed the pallor of fear from her face, replacing it with a rosy glow, but her eyes were still wide open and staring into the abyss like a deer in headlights.

"Go check for Morgan at the icehouse again," Jewelia directed Hannah.

"Right," Hannah said.

But when she got to the icehouse, there was still no sign of Morgan. She walked back to the manor, a feeling of defeat in her chest. When she entered the kitchen, she could tell that Jewelia, Wendy, and Old Man Adams read her disappointment immediately.

Jewelia stood up. "Do not despair, my dear. It may seem like nothing is happening, but on another level it surely is. We must never doubt our ability to effect change, while also remembering that each soul has its own path to walk."

"But there must be something else we can do," Hannah said, wringing her hands in frustration. "Wait, I know! I'll go check Morgan's apartment. Maybe there will be clues."

"Okay, but first give us a hand," Jewelia replied. "Let's bring Jezebelle upstairs to a bedroom so she'll be more comfortable."

The four of them carried Jezebelle up the stairs to the closest bedroom and gently laid her down on the bed. As Hannah turned for the door, Jewelia reached out to her. "Be careful. I worry about you going to Morgan's apartment alone."

"It's nearly midnight, I'll go with you," Old Man Adams offered, putting his hand on Hannah's shoulder.

They quickly descended the stairs together, swiftly making it out to the car. The rain had subsided, although the ground was still wet.

They wound their way down the drive and out through the tall iron gate that marked the edge of the manor grounds. The road ran straight through the darkness toward the village of Maple Hollow. The island was shaped like a key, with Skye Manor in the more circular top area and the town clustered farther down the shank, side roads branching off into the notches. Given the late hour, the town was quiet and deserted when they arrived, the only light coming from the glowing lanterns on the elegant black lamp posts. When they stopped in front of Maple Moon, the shop and the apartment above it were dark, and the doors were locked.

"She's not here either," Old Man Adams said.

Hannah began to feel increasingly uneasy. First it was Jewelia who had disappeared, and she had found her through pumpkin magick. But now Morgan was gone, and the pumpkin magick wasn't working.

CHAPTER EIGHT

THE DISCOVERY

At a loss, Hannah and Old Man Adams walked back to the car. "Can you drop me off at the library?" Hannah asked.

"Are you sure you'll be okay?" he said in a tone of caution.

"I just want to check in with Ashlin," Hannah explained. "She's been researching what we learned from the grimoire about the Dark One of Phantasm, the Illusionix. I need to see if she found anything useful."

They drove together down the tree-lined streets of the village toward the library.

"Why don't you see if she's still there before I leave?" Adams suggested as they pulled up. "Jewelia won't be happy if I show up at the manor alone."

Hannah agreed. When they arrived, she hopped out. "Okay, I'll be right back!"

"I'll be here!" he said.

Hannah climbed the steps to the front door of the old Victorian house, which had been designated a historical site and made into a library many years ago. Disconcertingly, she found the door ajar. She walked slowly in, the door gently creaking, and then her mouth gaped open at what she saw. It was Ashlin, sitting in a lotus pose, but she was levitating off the ground. From the door, Hannah could see her back. Ashlin's arms were stretched out, with her hands resting on each knee. Her head was upright, neck long, back straight. Surrounding her, floating off the shelves, were the books. It seemed like she was controlling them with her mind. It was as if they were getting caught up in a mystical net of ethereal fabric that suspended them in air. Some of them flipped open their pages, others waited for examination.

Hannah was mystified. She knew that Ashlin was the keeper of the island's wisdom, as Old Man Adams put it, but she'd just thought that meant she worked at the library. She didn't actually think it meant more than that, but clearly it did. Jewelia's cryptic letter to her before she came to Maple Hollow had said how the women of the island all had powers, but Hannah hadn't yet pondered who that might refer to besides Morgan and Wendy, or even what their powers might be.

She didn't want to interrupt Ashlin's magick, so she quietly retreated behind the door. After some time, the books all returned to their resting places and Ashlin slowly descended to the floor. She got up and turned to exit the library, not seeing Hannah in the doorway.

Hannah was suddenly unsure what to do. She knew Old Man Adams was waiting for her, so without thinking she quickly headed back out to the car.

"All set?" he asked.

"Yes," Hannah said with some hesitation, not revealing what she had seen. She was even more fascinated now by Ashlin. She wanted to know more about her powers and what her abilities were, but there wasn't time right now.

When they got back to the manor, they both went straight upstairs to check on Jezebelle. Wendy was sitting next to the bed, watching over her friend with a look of concern on her face. "Jewelia's sleeping, we're taking shifts," she told them.

"How's she doing?" Old Man Adams asked.

"Come closer," Wendy whispered to both of them. "I want to show you something." She lightly picked up one of Jezebelle's hands. It was cold and limp, her creamy skin taking on a hue of lavender in the light.

"What is it?" Hannah asked.

"Her fingernails...there's something there."

Hannah leaned in for a closer look. Underneath Jezebelle's fingernails was something that made her nails a reddish blue. But she couldn't quite tell what the substance was.

"I see," she said. "What do you think it is?"

"I don't know. It looks...purple," Wendy said.

"Purple? Hmm, fabric from the furniture in the parlor perhaps?" suggested Old Man Adams. "Although I don't think that would stain."

"It must be something else," Wendy said. "Maybe the fruit from the dinner? I did serve dragon fruit and pomegranates."

"It's possible," Hannah said.

"I knew I shouldn't have brought her with me," Wendy said, looking with remorse at Jezebelle. "I felt bad for her. She's been going through a difficult time and I thought getting away from it all would be good for her."

"How well do you know Jezebelle?" Hannah asked.

"Unfortunately, not all that well," Wendy conceded. "Now that I think about it, she actually was quite insistent that she come with me. I figured she was just curious."

"So…Jezebelle wanted to come with you?" Old Man Adams asked.

"It was all she was talking about the past few weeks," Wendy said, gently placing Jezebelle's hand back on her chest.

As they watched her, Jezebelle remained still as a ghost.

"What do you mean, all she talked about? What did she say?" Hannah finally asked.

"Recently she's been very chatty about beauty remedies. That's mostly all she talks about anyway, but she'd become particularly obsessed with specific ingredients that go beyond the realm of cosmetics into things that might induce more of a permanent state of beautification," Wendy said slowly.

"Like what?"

"Apparently, some really elusive plants that are not common out west, but can be found, however rare, in the northeastern states."

"Do you remember what any of them were called?" Old Man Adams inquired, frowning in concentration. "We do have a greenhouse here, you know, with many rare plants, flowers, and herbs."

"Of course, I used herbs for the entrees and the balm, but I hadn't put together till now that perhaps Jezebelle had a secret interest in the greenhouse for other reasons."

"She must have known about the greenhouse," Hannah said.

"I'm really beginning to think she did," Wendy replied.

"It's pretty late. I think we all need to get some rest," Old Man Adams said. "I'll watch Jezebelle for the next few hours until Jewelia gets up. You two should go to bed."

Wendy and Hannah made their way to their bedrooms and promptly went to bed.

***

Hannah fell into a deep sleep. She was exhausted from worry and her body finally surrendered to the stupor it longed for.

She found herself running out of the back of Morgan's shop along the leaf-strewn stone sidewalk. But once she got to the front of the shop, she realized she was no longer on the ground level. The sidewalk had dropped below her and she was now on the outside of the building on the second floor, except her feet were occupying a very narrow space along the edge of a stone wall that had been carved away. There was barely enough room for her feet between the stone wall and the drop-off edge. When she realized this, she tried to walk backward, but lost her footing and grasped for the front of the building. There were wooden shutters attached to the exterior and she clung to them with her hands, attempting to press her whole body and chest against them, bonding herself with the building. She dug her fingernails into the wood crevices, but the rotten wood began to give way. It separated from the building, pulling toward her, and she had to shift her weight and toss the shutter she clung to off to the left. Just as that happened, the larger shutters on the building began to open like large doors, and she saw that inside was a brightly lit restaurant and bar. She felt relief that perhaps she could just walk in from her level and not have to struggle, clinging to the outside.

One dream blended into another and she found herself running into the foyer of the manor. Once she arrived, she was greeted by a gray kitten.

"Wixby!" Hannah yelped, running toward the kitten. "It's been so long. I thought you'd gone!" she exclaimed.

"Don't you know I'm always with you," Wixby said in a sweet, lispy voice.

"You must help me. Morgan is missing and Jezebelle is sick!" Hannah delivered the news as fast as she could.

"Morgan?!" Wixby's eyes widened into large orbs as he jumped into her lap. "Oh no!" he exclaimed, tapping his tail harder. "Wait...who's Jezebelle?" he tilted his head.

"Oh, she's a friend of Wendy's. Remember Wendy, Jewelia's old friend?"

"Yes, hmm...have you checked with Morgan's cats?" Wixby asked in a matter-of-fact kind of tone.

"Oh, I hadn't thought of that. Of course!" Hannah exclaimed, and then immediately woke up.

When Hannah awoke, she thought about her old job playing piano at the Midnight Lounge in Morningside, her hometown out west where she'd lived before moving in with Jewelia on the island. Losing her job there had been a catalyst to come to Maple Hollow in the first place. Hannah's stomach knotted a bit when she thought about those final moments when Miss Gardenia laid her off. Even though it happened a few years ago, the resonance of the unpleasantness seemed to still be stored inside her body. Then her mind went to Morgan, everything that had happened the night before, and how Morgan's shop had been all locked up and dark. Part of her was anticipating another struggle, another roadblock in her life. She wondered if she was ready to meet this new challenge head-on.

Chapter Nine

THE LEGACY

SEPTEMBER 10, 2009

She was so happy to have seen Wixby again, her frequent dream companion from the days when she was searching for Jewelia. Grabbing the journal she had procured from Morgan's shop from her bedside table, Hannah began frantically recording the fleeting dream memory. It had a smooth black velvet cover, pleasing to the tips of her fingers as they grazed across it. On the front cover, etched with white stitching, was a mystical eye. Hannah appreciated this design because when she reached for her journal in the middle of the night, she could tell the front from the back and knew she'd be writing on the page in the correct direction. This helped when trying to read it later, in the light of day.

It never ceased to amaze her how quickly she would forget where she was in her dreams, what she had experienced, who she was with, or what she saw and what she learned. She had always enjoyed recording her dreams, but ever since discovering her family lineage, her personal power, and the otherworld, she'd begun to pay even closer attention. Morgan had told her the best way to capture dreams was to write them down as soon as you woke up. Preferably before getting out of bed, moving around too much, turning the light on, or anything else.

Hannah's dreams had become even more vivid since moving to the manor. She had learned the importance of listening, even to the mundane ones. Dreams truly did hold messages for her, and were there as her guidance and own wisdom.

As she wrapped up her summary of meeting Wixby, she suddenly realized that with Morgan gone, there would be no one to feed her cats! She would have to go to Morgan's apartment daily until they could figure out where she'd gone and why.

Hannah rose from her bed and walked down the hallway to the room they had put Jezebelle in. Jewelia was now the one sitting at the bedside.

"Hannah, come in, love," Jewelia said when she saw her at the door.

"Good morning." Hannah entered and took a seat on a small bench. "I had a dream last night about Wixby."

"You did?" Jewelia replied.

"It made me worried about Merlin and Milu. With Morgan gone, who's going to feed them?" Hannah asked.

"Oh love, you know you're right. What would I have done without Mr. Adams to feed Midnight while I was gone?" she said, then paused. "I think Morgan has a spare key to her apartment hidden in one of the trees around the shop."

"Oh, that's perfect. I'll ride over there this morning and see if I can find it."

"That would be so good of you, love," Jewelia replied. "I will keep a close eye on Jezebelle. I know it's a lot of watching and waiting, but I'm certain this is not something medical doctors can help us with."

Hannah nodded. She had no intention of involving authorities or outsiders and trusted Jewelia's judgment of the situation, regardless of how unclear Jezebelle's affliction was.

Then her eyes were drawn to a large photo on the wall. It was tattered and worn, but it called to her.

"Who is this?" she asked, pointing to the person who stood at the end of a line. It was summertime and there was a group of young women standing with their arms wrapped around one another, the open water of the sea sprawling behind them.

"That's Morgan, and that's me," Jewelia replied, gesturing at two of the young women in the picture.

"Morgan?" Hannah exclaimed. "She looks so young," she mused without thinking, then followed up with, "and so do you!"

Jewelia smiled. "And that's Wendy. That was the summer we came into our power," she recalled. "It was a difficult yet wonderful time."

"Why was it difficult?" Hannah asked.

"You see, my love, when we discover something about ourselves, we aren't always ready to accept it. Many times it means giving up something else." She paused.

"What did you have to give up?" Hannah asked.

"Discovering our calling meant recognizing that our purpose to humanity was much larger than ourselves. That we must acknowledge our new role and bravely step in, leaving behind old ideas, judgments, and fears. Realizing we aren't like everyone else is both empowering and alienating. It can be distressing and lonely if we don't fully lean into it. Sometimes we must let go of parts of ourselves that no longer serve us, so we can serve others."

Hannah was curious how her aunt had navigated that part of her life, and how Morgan and Wendy had as well. She began to wonder if she was at a similar crossroads. Her gaze drifted beyond the photo to the various mirrors that were hung around it, all of different shapes and sizes.

"Aunt Jewelia, why do you have so many mirrors here at the manor?" Hannah asked carefully. "Where did they all come from?"

She had always wondered about the mirrors. When she'd first arrived at Skye Manor, she had noticed with awe that the walls, especially of the staircase and upstairs hallway, were filled with thousands of different mirrors. Some were so large it would take a team of men to move, and others were so small you could tuck them in your pocket and take them with you. Initially, she'd wondered if they were just an unusual collection, something motivated by vanity, standing at the ready to reaffirm an earthly obsession with perception. This was certainly what Jezebelle used mirrors for.

"These mirrors have accumulated over many years," Jewelia replied. "There've been some added since I've been an adult, but most were here before me. Just like the pumpkin patch, the mirrors in Skye Manor are all very special. There are none like them in all the world. They were brought by our ancestors to the island of Maple Hollow when they established the town as part of our family legacy," she went on, her fingers passing over the ornate gilded metal on the wall. The glass of the mirrors was bordered with intertwining Celtic knotwork, forged into the steel unlike anything Hannah had ever seen before.

She thought back over her life, instances of mirrors passing through her mind as if she were standing at a depot watching a train speed by. Her experiences with mirrors had always left her wondering. When she was younger, she would stare into the mirror in her bedroom for hours, looking beyond her reflection into the space beyond the glass, where her image seemed to dissolve and her eyes would begin to see things beyond the obvious. She almost felt like she could see into a world that others often missed, even though it was right there in front of them. The thought had briefly crossed her mind that mirrors might be a doorway to somewhere else. The pumpkins had called to her since she was a child. They were her first portal. Now she wanted to master the mirrors.

"Can you show me more?" she asked.

"Of course, my love," Aunt Jewelia obliged. "Come with me," she said as she rose.

Chapter Ten

THE MIRRORS

She followed Aunt Jewelia down the stairs into the foyer, her heels clicking on the hardwood floors, her long velvet dress sashaying around her ankles.

"Choose any mirror you wish," Aunt Jewelia said as she waved her hand toward the walls that towered above them. Mirrors of all shapes and sizes crammed the space.

Hannah approached the wall and stood face to face with a round mirror that was exactly her height. It was easy to choose this one; it called to her and drew her in, but it wasn't black like the ones at the party, so Hannah wasn't sure how to start.

"Now, I want you to relax your mind," Aunt Jewelia said. "Pretend as if you are about to fall into a deep sleep, but with your eyes open. Don't look into the mirror, look through it."

Hannah stood as still as possible and stared straight into the mirror. Somehow, the longer she stared, the more she started to lose sight of herself. She tried to resist blinking for as long as possible, but each time, she would succumb to the urge and have to start once again. Catching herself staring at one eye or the other, she would shift her gaze to between her eyes. The curves of her eyebrows and the sides of her nose cast a shadow that, the longer she stared, began to look almost like a butterfly. Its dark wings spread between her eyes, blazing like an awakened third eye.

Her face became a blurry apparition and her vision seemed to pass beyond the reflection of her pupils into someplace deeper. It was as if by concentrating on her reflection she was able to pass into another reality. It reminded her of those trick-of-the-eye puzzles where you can't see anything initially but a bunch of fuzzy lines. But when she shifted and relaxed her gaze, no longer looking in the same way, the space around her reflection began to destabilize.

"Keep looking through," Jewelia said, encouraging her.

Hannah held her ground, all her focus on looking past herself in the glass. Then she blinked, and suddenly she snapped completely out of the trance she had induced herself into. She was back looking at her own face, seeing all of her eyelashes out of place and small marks on her skin. "I lost it," she said begrudgingly.

"Don't worry, love, it takes practice," Jewelia reassured her. "You will master the mirror eventually. It just takes time. Remember, Hannah, when we look into the mirror, we can see beyond this world. It is a world where our physical form begins to melt into the ether of what we once were and what we will become again. It is a netherworld of knowing, a place that doesn't require our effort; we just are. We are part of a oneness only we can remember, individual yet whole, part of everything and nothing." She gazed up at the wall of mirrors. "Once we achieve this state, we can never go back. We wouldn't want to. It is a state of pure knowing, enveloped by the light of what we truly are, deep down in the depths of our core. Unfettered by who we think we should be, who anyone else tells us to be, or what we on this Earth think with our physical minds we want to be."

"How did you learn all of this?" Hannah asked, dropping onto a nearby bench in frustration.

"All of our family's abilities are passed down through the generations," Jewelia said simply. "You can't expect to have full control of your abilities all at once. They come in time. Most people don't ever get this close to knowing what they are capable of. You are one of the lucky ones, Hannah, that now you know. I'd like to show you something else." Jewelia beckoned to her as she started down the hall toward the library. Midnight ran behind them as they stepped through the door under the stairs.

Once inside the library, Jewelia paused. "There used to be many of us," she explained, pulling an old photo album from the shelf. "These are our ancestors, Hannah," she said, flipping through the large burnished picture book, the pages brown and slightly torn on the edges, the pictures sepia and ancient.

Hannah peered into the solemn eyes of her long-lost family. There were pictures of the manor, with people gathered around in front or back. The grounds were so new then, it seemed, the foliage not as large, the bushes small. She began to wonder about the other families of the island. "How much do you know about Ashlin and her family?" she asked.

"Ah yes, Ashlin. Her family name is Aldona, as you know, which means Wise Elder. They are the keepers of the wisdom, which in this world translates on the practical level to librarians. Ashlin's parents named her after the word 'Aislin,' which is Celtic for 'dream.'"

"Do our family paths intertwine? Did they have a dream calling, as well as keeping the wisdom?" Hannah asked searchingly.

"They very well could. There is a reason all the families came to this island together, and I'm sure the connections are as endless as a spider's web. All the women of Maple Hollow have layers of experience when their gifts awaken; a series of portals, each layer deeper than the next."

They stood in silence, staring at the old photos. "They whisper to us," Jewelia said softly into Hannah's ear. "It's our calling now," she added resolutely, louder. "Over time our family has dwindled down, and now it is just us. There used to be hundreds, thousands of us, but the dark forces were too strong, and we began to lose the fight. I even wanted to give up the fight at times. I felt I couldn't go on. That is why I had to reach out to you, love." She placed her hand gently on Hannah's shoulder again.

Hannah's eyes lit up as she remembered that it was in fact through a mirror at the manor that she was finally able to read the cryptic letter Jewelia sent her before she disappeared. What at first was illegible had become legible. Perhaps she had already unknowingly tapped the ancestral mirror magick ability of the Skye family. But she certainly had not mastered it.

"It's true! I read your letter using the mirror," she said. "That's how I figured it out. Well, Midnight helped."

"Of course he did, and I'm so glad! I knew it was time for you to know, and for me to reach out beyond myself and not feel that I had to do this work alone anymore. Together we are meant to co-create, to fight the malevolent energies. That is why I wrote the letter backward and charmed it."

"How did you learn to do that, anyway? Can I learn to write backward, too?" Hannah asked.

"You don't need to learn, because you already know. All you need to do...is remember. It is called mirror writing. It is a rare ability, passed down genetically through the women of our lineage. Very few people are able to read or write backward. I knew once your mind was open it would reveal itself to you. We are also gifted with extra senses, and the ability to perceive things others cannot. Some call it synesthesia. Have you ever seen colors in your mind when you hear music?"

"I have!" Hannah said with excitement. "I thought it was just me."

"I knew the letter would lead you to the mirror. Which would lead you back to yourself. This is why the manor is full of mirrors. Mirrors are our portal back to ourselves. So many on Earth feel it is just a reflection; they look in the mirror and sigh and worry about what they see. They just look at the surface, but they don't look *through it*. It is a trick of the eye and a trick of the mind, these mirrors. They only reveal what we are ready to see. Yet it is through them that we can truly see, but only when we are ready. Beyond the mirror is beyond the veil, taking us toward realms where we truly can embody, with our spirit, our highest calling. You have heard the call, my love."

"I can see how mirrors trick us into looking just at the surface," Hannah mused. "We come to expect the reflection. It's almost self-fulfilling."

"Mirrors are an invitation to our divine connection, a pathway through the glass," Jewelia said. "A dimensional doorway that we can casually pass by if we don't heed its echo. But we are different; we know what lies beyond. We know what we are and we use the mirror to embrace this, to transform ourselves, to lighten our paths. It doesn't matter the size of the mirror, or the shape. In fact, it can be found in nature as well."

"Yes, I've often wondered about water as a mirror."

Jewelia nodded. "When you peer into water, a clear still pond, a bathtub filled to the brim, a puddle on a street corner, your morning mug of coffee...these too all have their mirrors. Mirrors into the beyond. We can help others see these mirrors and find themselves within them. This is what we are here to do as Healers, my love. The mirrors are our alchemy, our magick. Along with the pumpkins and the patch, we have so many powers at our fingertips. So many tools with which we can manifest. There are so many things we can do with mirrors. We can trap good energy in mirrors to take with us. When the moon is at its fullest, I take some mirrors outside and infuse them with the moonlight. But be forewarned...with knowledge comes power, so we must be careful. All portals carry risks. There are those, like the Dream Haunters, that cross dimensions looking for opportunities to take advantage of lost souls. You never know who you might let out or in," she said, raising one eyebrow.

"So, mirrors are really the hidden magick around us all the time," Hannah said slowly. "They exist mostly unacknowledged in this world. People are taught to look into them to see themselves, so that is what they do, and ultimately what they see. But what they don't realize is that the reflection they see is in fact an illusion, a figment of this reality, and that there is more than what they see in the mirror."

She closed the photo album and picked up one of the larger mirrors. As she stared through and beyond it, Hannah understood all that she was sharing with her aunt in a way she never had before.

They left the library together. Hannah felt the mirrors watching her as they walked along the dark hallway, shadows chasing their shadows.

Chapter Eleven

THE ILLUSIONIX

They entered the kitchen together to find Wendy busy scurrying about cooking breakfast. Ingredients, bowls, and spoons were strewn across the spacious counters. Glowing lanterns hung from heavy crisscrossed wooden beams that soared above their heads.

"Where were you two?" Wendy asked.

"In the library, talking about mirrors," Hannah replied.

"Ah, mirrors," Wendy said thoughtfully. "Such a profound concept."

"What's your theory on mirrors, Wendy?" Hannah asked as she grabbed some plates from the cupboard.

"Well," she began, "on the physical plane, the mirror only shows us one side, right? We only see our material form, onto which our mind immediately projects everything it believes. The way we are 'supposed' to be. Which is often based on what *we see* out in the world with our visual eyes."

"That is so true," Hannah said, setting the table and taking a seat next to Jewelia.

"But the reality is that we are not just our physical form. We are not meant to be the reflection of others, and what we try to emulate about others, is merely a false reflection. It is not their true spirit either," Wendy continued as she served up pumpkin spice oatmeal to Hannah and Jewelia, a bowl in each hand. "In my opinion, our existence is a duality. On the one side is the human form, and on the other, our spirit. We constantly have to balance the two streams of input. Our mind says one thing, our spirit another."

"Interesting." Hannah thought of Jezebelle and the inner feelings of inadequacy she had initially felt at her appearance.

"Only when we look beyond the mirror, through to the other side, can we then understand our true nature. Our wiser, expansive self that spans far beyond the confines of our physical body. That self knows all the answers we seek," Jewelia said as Wendy opened the stove and reached in for a hot bread pan with a large potholder.

"Agreed. Since we have a foot in both worlds, it's our task here on Earth to find that balance, to learn how to exist while honoring both worlds. But even more important is learning how to embody our higher self, which means not judging ourselves based on the reflections of others." Wendy drew a large bread knife from the wooden knife block and began slicing up the warm bread. "Everyone has their own journey. We cannot see behind anyone's mirror but our own. The ultimate test is to not believe the reflection, to look beyond the mirror's surface. To realize there is so much more."

This resonated with Hannah, and she realized that as much as Jezebelle had appeared to check all the boxes of the "perfect" appearance, she too was suffering inside.

"You're right. When we look in the mirror, sometimes we don't even see ourselves. We see what we think others see. This leads us into a cycle of comparison where we focus immediately on the parts we don't like. I know I do sometimes," Hannah admitted.

"And that's perfectly natural, love," Jewelia said in consolation. "But that's an illusion in itself."

"No one can ever see us the way we see ourselves, and we can never truly see others the way they see themselves," Wendy said, raising an eyebrow.

"Yes, perception is a puzzle, never truly revealing itself," Jewelia chimed in.

"We all have to exist here on this earthly plane, in the bodies our spirits are in." Wendy passed bread to Hannah and Jewelia. "But we have a choice to allow our spiritual selves to emerge, to cast off the mind games we inherit or acquire, and to choose instead to stay centered between *our* eyes, within *our* mind's eye, sitting at the seat of *our* soul instead."

"I think I know what you mean. The whole world is so caught up with images of how we should look. In fact, every aspect of ourselves is pressurized into a laundry list of *shoulds*. It's exhausting to constantly try to meet all those expectations," Hannah lamented. "I can see how if we allow that external pressure to dictate our actions, we're actually giving away our power. We're in a sense putting our own worth and value into question. By elevating the status quo, whether it's about accomplishments, beauty, or other societal standards, we essentially relinquish our true worth. Our own insecurity convinces us to discard what we actually hold in the depths of our soul to be true."

"Yes, yes, exactly, love." Jewelia took a sip from her mug. "That is the challenge right there. And as I'm sure you've come to realize, mirrors also operate on multiple additional planes. Our minds also have a mirror within them: our conscious and our subconscious. We must merge the two opposing aspects of our mind. So much of what we perceive about the world is rooted in the subconscious, and we are totally unaware of its influence. It is only through embracing our shadow that we stand a chance of integrating the two halves of the whole, to gain a more universal perspective. This is our challenge as well."

"It's interesting to think about mirrors as a metaphor for our consciousness," Hannah said, wiping her buttery fingers on her napkin.

"Yes, this is part of the magick of mirrors." Jewelia smiled. "We can actually use them to see what we are hiding from ourselves. What we are holding in our subconscious. What we are unaware of that is influencing every moment of our existence."

"Ignorance is not bliss in this case. Being unaware does not relinquish our responsibility to see. We can go through our whole life and ignore what is beyond the mirror, but it is there the whole time nonetheless," Wendy remarked.

Hannah took a big gulp of her chai. "So, where do the Dream Haunters and Illusionix fit into all of this?"

"The Dream Haunters have the ability to sway us when we become weak in our fortitude. This can happen for a variety of reasons...incidental, astrological...but whatever the catalyst, they seize the opportunity," Jewelia explained. "They become the little voice in our head that reinforces the narrative of doubt, self-loathing, and hopelessness. They try to confirm for us our fears, that are in reality often not valid. They take advantage of us and capitalize on our weakness. The Illusionix work in the same way. Except they do their work through the mirrors. They are masters of deflection, and they attempt to rule reflection. They can manipulate what we see and what we think about what we see, taking away our agency and free will. They also are experts at making us forget about our universal selves."

Jewelia stood, gathered her dishes, and walked to the sink to gaze out the window at the grounds, brilliant in the late morning sun. "Just as the Dream Haunters want to convince you that your fears and nightmares are real and all that there is in your life, the Illusionix want to convince you that your reflection is real and all that there is. That this world, which is merely an illusion, is real. The Illusionix sway us to criticize our reflection, pick apart what we see, and also pass judgment on others as we negate our own worth. They are experts in 'never enough.' They invented the concept and work for it to take hold over the world. For the most part, they are very successful. But when we as humans decide to notice our spiritual selves, it dispels the facade. It cracks the veritable foundation of the mirror's illusion, destabilizing their hold on us. The more we become aware of our own duality and the nature of our existence, the less hold they have over us."

"They really do have our worst interest in mind, don't they?" Hannah observed. "It's hard enough in this life, then we have them to fight on top of it."

"Yes, but it is our calling really as Healers of the Hollow to help others navigate these dark places. To raise the spiritual intelligence of others of the true reality, and of the illusion. The more we can help others break free, the more we elevate the consciousness of the planet overall, freeing us all from the shackles of the unnecessary and actualizing our potential on this plane and beyond."

Hannah sat still, taking it all in. She could definitely see all the ways and times the Illusionix had walked at her side, even though she had not realized it before. And now she could see what they had done to Jezebelle. It was up to her now, as a Healer, to help Jezebelle break free of her captivity, her trap within the illusion.

But in order to help Jezebelle separate from the illusion, she had to release herself as well.

Chapter Twelve

THE SHOP

Hannah stepped outside and grabbed her bike. Before doing anything else, she had to head into town to feed Morgan's cats. The cool autumn air filled her nostrils. There was a gentle sound, like a rolling wave, as the maple trees swayed on the soft breeze, releasing golden leaves that cascaded down from their branches and landed softly on the ground below.

When she arrived at the metaphysical shop, she parked her bike near two small bistro tables that each featured a large pumpkin in the middle ringed by small glistening lights. The first floor of the building consisted of shop windows, within which were wonderfully gathered decorations: books, plants, pumpkins, candles with glowing flames, colored bottles, and round glowing glass orbs. Milu, Morgan's black cat, was lying in one of the windows, his silky fur soaking up the morning sun. She looked up at the second floor, where three windows spanned the width of the building. Above them was the large sign that said *Maple Moon*. And winding up the edge of the building to cross the tops of the windows were tiny fairy lights, wrapped around a long garland of dried forest material made of gathered golden leaves, fronds, and flowers. Two hanging lanterns were suspended from the building's front.

Jewelia had told her where to look for the key. Hannah took inventory of the large maple trees that bordered the shop. A tall maple tree stood on either side of the building, leaves gently undulating with the light breeze. It was as if the shop itself and the sidewalks around it had been built around the trees, preserving them where they stood. She wasn't sure which tree to check, but one in particular had a distinct notch in it where the branches parted near the trunk.

As she got closer, she could see there was an opening. Hannah slowly reached her hand inside, hoping nothing would bite her or crawl up her arm. To her surprise, her fingers touched something soft. She grabbed it and brought it out into the light. It was a small velvet pouch. And lo and behold, inside…was a key, and a small note that read, *i gcás éigeandála*.

Hannah pulled out her phone and started to type the cryptic phrase into the search engine. She wasn't surprised when she discovered it meant literally "in case of emergency" in Irish. Below the phrase was a set of symbols she didn't recognize.

Hannah went to the front door of the shop, placed the key into the lock, and turned it slowly. As she stepped inside, Morgan's gray cat, Merlin, came prancing up to greet her, chatting and meowing as he went.

"Merlin, are you hungry?" Hannah said as she petted his head. "Let's go and see what we can find for you two." Merlin followed close at her heels in anticipation.

Hannah had visited Morgan's shop many times but had never been behind the curtain to the back room before, nor to the apartment above it where Morgan lived. But she and Jewelia had now agreed it was time to take matters into their own hands. As she crossed behind the curtain, her curiosity and anticipation grew. She had always wondered what was in the back room.

Her eyes feasted upon an elaborate wall of trinkets. Near her feet were stacks of domed containers in jeweled colors, lined with beads. Above that was an ornate but sturdy wooden table. The top could scarcely be seen as it was so filled with small trays, jars, candles, mini plates, bowls, discarded sage sticks, small brass containers, twine, and wax intermingled with glowing orbs and crystals.

Rising from the table, against the wall, were shelves that reached to the ceiling. On either side, they were crested with round knobs. Each shelf was crammed with small volumes, statues, and more multi-colored jars with cork lids, each one with a cryptic label. Some were deep blue, some bright red, others gold and brown.

A large lantern hung next to the shelves, suspended from the ceiling. No doubt it was placed to illuminate the crowded shelves when Morgan needed to retrieve an ingredient. The rest of the wall was filled with additional shelves that appeared almost like branches of a tree; they unevenly fought for space on the wall, each one more crowded than the next, sprawling up and across toward the ceiling.

She had to find Merlin and Milu's food, and she hadn't seen it yet in this room. *Morgan must keep it up in her apartment*, she thought. She spotted and approached a closed door. It slowly creaked open when she pulled the handle, and before her Hannah saw a dark staircase leading up. She slowly climbed the stairs.

At the top, she entered the most enchanting room she had ever seen aside from the library at the manor. The sun's rays gleamed through the windows, illuminating the cozy scene. There was a large fireplace in the middle of the room, surrounded by white and gray stones. Hanging upside down from the mantle were stalks of grain and dried flowers. The mantle itself was dark brown wood and held a large brass urn and several tall candles in silver candlesticks.

On either side of the fireplace, were tall bookshelves built into the walls. Filling each shelf were thick volumes covered with a moss that coated most of the exposed wood of the shelves. The volumes were all rose, powder blue, forest green, and orange in color, each with different flowers or herbs drawn on the spines.

Above the fireplace, was a large gilded frame. Inside was a painting of a woman sitting by the sea. Her dress and hair were flowing freely. The sun was setting and seagulls crossed the sky.

The other wall was filled with pieces of paper that looked aged, their ends turned and cracked. They were pinned to the wall in a haphazard manner, strings of mossy twine stretched across them. The floor in front of the fireplace was crowded with baskets filled with dried flowers and herbs, next to stacked books. Flower pots bursting with tall purple flowers. In front of the fireplace was a large tattered but comfortable-looking chair.

As soon as Hannah entered, Milu came running in from behind her and jumped up on the chair.

"Is that your chair?" Hannah asked him, as he proudly sat staring up at her with his seafoam eyes.

He did not reply but tapped his tail, watching and waiting for his meal.

"Of course, I'm getting to it," she said, remembering why she had come there in the first place.

As she spun around, she saw a small kitchen area. The counter was chock full of tins of tea and large black canisters, one of which had painted glowing cat eyes.

"There it is," she said, as she reached for it.

Merlin, circling her ankles, raised his paw in approval, then raced over to a cozy window seat. Side by side were two small bowls, one with Merlin's name and one with Milu's. Hannah filled the bowls with the crunchy kibble from the canister. Merlin immediately began to munch in glee, filling his hungry belly. Milu watched from the chair like a wise tiger waiting patiently for the right time to spring on his prey. Perhaps he was older, wiser, and patient. He'd let Merlin get his fill first.

"C'mon, Milu," Hannah said tapping the bowl, trying to entice him. "Merlin's going to eat it all if you don't come quick."

But Milu didn't budge. He just sat stoically in the chair, watching.

"I know I'm not Morgan, but I'm here to help until she comes back," Hannah said, placing the canister back on the counter. She suddenly remembered what Wixby had suggested in her dream. She looked directly at Milu and asked, "Do you know where Morgan is?"

After sharing a deep mutual gaze, he leapt off the chair and onto a stack of books near the fireplace. She noticed that behind where he had been sitting on the chair was a tattered volume, with a pen holding open a page near the middle. She grabbed the volume and took his place in the chair, leaning back against the worn cushion. When she opened to where the pen was, she noticed it wasn't a book at all, but a journal. It was filled with handwriting. *Could this be Morgan's handwriting?* Hannah wondered. *Could this be Morgan's journal?*

The thought crossed her mind about how she would feel if someone else read her dream journal. But at the same time, she needed to figure out what had happened to Morgan, and the curiosity and pull she felt to now read her journal was irresistible. With Milu watching carefully over her, Hannah began to flip the lined pages.

Some were filled with sketches, diagrams, and plans written in an almost hasty and messy hand. Others with long paragraphs written in neat, flowy penmanship stretching to the edges of the pages. Hannah noticed that the last date entered was August 18th, which struck her as odd since that was over three weeks ago.

She had grown closer to Morgan over the past two years in Maple Hollow, especially after what she, Jewelia, and Morgan had experienced with the Dream Haunters. They had suffered yet triumphed together. And meeting Morgan had opened up a new world for Hannah, into realms unknown. Morgan's guidance awakened in her an inner power, one that she had long forgotten but never truly lost. Her disappearance weighed heavily on Hannah.

She wanted to dwell longer in the room. There was something so cozy and comforting about Morgan's small abode above the shop. But she knew she should get back to the manor and check on Jezebelle. Hannah closed the journal, leaving the pen in place, and set it carefully back on the chair. She bent down and petted Milu's head, then walked over to the window seat and petted Merlin's head.

"I'll be back tomorrow, and the next day if need be," she reassured the cats as they looked up at her. Then she turned and walked back down to the shop.

After locking the front door behind her, Hannah retrieved her bike and headed back through the quaint and cheerful streets of Maple Hollow, all the while missing Morgan.

CHAPTER THIRTEEN

THE SHORE

Hannah arrived back at the manor and went upstairs to check on Jezebelle. She seemed about the same. Hannah reached out to hold Jezebelle's hand, but when she did, she noticed that the stain was not just under her nails anymore. The tips of her fingers were now all a dark purple as well. Not just the nailbeds, but the tops and pads of her actual fingers too. Hannah stopped and stared in contemplation.

"This looks much worse," she said out loud. "What caused this, Jezebelle? What happened to you?" But Jezebelle didn't reply. Her eyes were fixed and her face expressionless. Hannah began to wonder if she could hear her at all.

She headed back downstairs to the kitchen. After heating up some soup and slurping it down, she left the manor and walked toward the shore. She knew it would help her gain a different perspective. Being out in nature, especially by open water, always had a way of resetting her nervous system. She had read once that anywhere water moves, whether it be a waterfall, crashing wave, or running river, ions are released into the air that have a positive biochemical reaction on one's mood.

When she arrived at the rocky shore just outside the woods, she immediately noticed how calm the sea was. It was like a plate of glass, so still that the trees that bordered it were duplicated in its surface. She could not help but notice the synchronicity. Just this morning she was discussing water as a mirror with Jewelia, and here in nature was another mirror presenting itself. Showing her how vast and intertwined it all was.

Hannah tucked her curls behind her ear as the wind picked up her hair. A large dragonfly appeared above her head as she walked; it seemed to levitate in front of her as if to beckon her attention. As soon as she noticed it and smiled, it flew off into the nearby trees.

Hannah gazed out across the water, the sun reflecting off the surface like shiny diamonds. She had come to commune with the sea, to use the water to scry for answers. She found a small pool she could access by sitting on a large rock. Her worry about Morgan weighed heavily on her heart. She picked up a small pebble and dropped it in the shallow pool of water. In her mind she called upon her spirit guides to assist her. She carefully watched the ripples of the water. Images of waving tree branches shimmered across her vision as she sat in silence.

Time was moving so fast for her lately. She began to wonder why she was bothering to check clocks at all, since whenever she did, it seemed to always be the same time. And lately, throughout the day, no matter the random activities she might be doing, she always seemed to look at the clock precisely at 11:11 or 1:11, 2:22, 3:33, or 5:55. She couldn't plan it, but she noticed it inevitably happened just the same. She had begun to feel it was a guiding force. Letting her know to keep going despite her vexation and worry.

CHAPTER FOURTEEN

THE SHADE

As Hannah walked along the shore, she listened for whispers from the beyond. Her thoughts revisited the nights before the 999 dinner, tracing all the plans she and Jewelia had made over the last year. Searching for any small details or clues she may have overlooked. Old Man Adams had fastidiously groomed the grounds for weeks. The estate was so massive it took him quite a long time to make the rounds. Each bush had been perfectly carved, each flower bed perfectly weeded in anticipation of the event. The manor's pumpkin patch, of course, was allowed to sprawl without any trimming, and the trees likewise had free reign as well to spread their roots into the ground as far as they could reach.

Because she was in charge of the meal planning and catering, Wendy had arrived in Maple Hollow before Jezebelle did. She had spent hours in the kitchen experimenting with recipes, the counters lined with a multitude of bottles that turned the space into a veritable laboratory of culinary experimentation. Hannah thought again about Wendy's magick. There was something so satisfying for Wendy about combining different ingredients, flavors, herbs, spices, and textures into one creative concoction. One day as Hannah watched her in the kitchen, Wendy had described cooking as "one of the real joys of earthly human existence."

They had put Ashlin in charge of the invites. Even though there were only six of them, it seemed appropriate given the significance of the event. Ashlin had selected the paper, designed the invitations, and carefully addressed each envelope, sealing them with the Skye Manor seal Jewelia had let her borrow, dipped in melted wax.

Hannah, with her acquired knowledge of the healing frequencies of sound, had naturally been in charge of the music. She'd selected an entire list of musical accompaniments for the evening, choosing pieces that were perfectly tuned to align the guests with the correct resonance for the portal.

Jewelia dubbed herself the master of ceremonies. She had researched how important the 999 cosmic portal was in their energetic evolution and the need for certain work to be done to advance their powers. This was the purpose of the mirror ceremony.

Deep in her thoughts, she had hardly noticed she had wandered past the shore, into the forest and toward the icehouse. She mulled over the dates in Morgan's diary, the eclipse earlier this summer and the celestial significance of September 9th. With each Mercury retrograde, Hannah knew, the Dream Haunters were busy trapping unsuspecting dreamers in their nightmares. There had been three retrogrades in 2008, and two earlier this year. They were now in the third. Ever since she'd discovered the vulnerability of these time periods, she'd kept a close watch on the astrological calendar. She always circled the dates on the calendar in her bedroom. And this time was no different. She had felt the shift as the retroshade was activated, before the retrograde commenced on September 7th.

Today was September 10th, and it would be Mercury retrograde until the 29th. Hannah knew in her gut what this meant. It was time once again to not only help those who were trapped but also to be mindful of herself. To pay close attention to her dreams and to heed their warnings. It was the only way she could be sure to circumvent the power of the Dream Haunters and not allow herself to ever be trapped again. And now there was a new danger, the Illusionix. It seemed to have made its way onto the island and was probably what had attacked Jezebelle. But Hannah felt no closer to understanding how it had all happened or why Morgan would suddenly go missing. Her thoughts raced with the possibility that even more people might be vulnerable during this time.

She suddenly remembered how the last entry in Morgan's journal was August 18th. That meant Morgan hadn't been recording her dreams for three weeks before the dinner. Why had she stopped? What if she had forgotten about the importance of recording them and had become trapped by the Dream Haunters?

***

That night, Hannah had a dream. She found herself in front of the bathroom mirror in her grandmother's house where she grew up. Without intention, she began to spin her right arm like she was winding up like a baseball pitcher. Each time she breathed out, she began to whisper, saying, *"Show me."* She got louder and stronger, saying *"Shhhhhhhooooowwwww mmmmmeeeeee,"* over and over. She started to feel as if she was conjuring something from within her. As if she was raising, summoning, something. She felt a bit disturbed, since she couldn't tell if this was something within her that was demanding something of her, or if she was demanding something of herself. Either way, it was urgent.

CHAPTER FIFTEEN

THE JOURNAL

SEPTEMBER 11, 2009

When Hannah woke up, it was still dark. She could hear the chirping of the crickets outside and knew it was still too early to get up. She told herself she should continue to rest, but her mind was running full speed.

She'd placed a pen as a placeholder inside her dream journal, which held open the pages where she last left off so she wouldn't have to fumble in the dark to find it. She didn't want to turn the light on, which would awaken morning chemicals that would wipe the memory from her mind like a swift wind, vanishing it all in an instant. She wrote down her dream as fast as her hand could, trying to keep up with her fading memory.

"It is in those wee moments at the break of awakening that we can harness our dreams' secrets," Morgan had told her. *"We cannot rely on our long-term memory. Dreams are fleeting and must be captured with intent. You will see. The more you practice, the more you will remember."*

Hannah had found she was right. She used to only remember the recurring dream she had about the pumpkin patch, which started long before she came to Skye Manor. But now, having discovered so much about herself and living with the magick of the island and the manor, she knew there was so much more to discover about her dreamworld. She was always anxious to find out more.

She had once asked Madame Morgan, *"If dreams are so important, why do we forget them so easily?"*

To which Madame Morgan had replied, *"Therein lies the mystery, dear. Dreams are there for us to discover. It is our duty to harness them. So much of what we need to know is hiding in plain sight, but standing behind the veil of perception. An illusion of inaccessibility, cloaking our very ability to access the knowledge. There is no need to fear this, but never relinquish your quest to harness it."*

But what if Morgan had begun to relinquish her quest? What if she had stopped harnessing her dream knowledge?

The word "illusion" echoed in Hannah's mind. Morgan had also told her that the right dream journal would be her companion, *"standing at the doorway between the worlds,"* and her confidant, *"listening intently to the whispers of the recesses of your mind."* She said the journal would hold safe her deepest thoughts, and that the puzzles the mind hides could be revealed through this process.

Hannah knew that she had already started the crucial process Morgan spoke about. That she was opening the veritable doorway to her dreamworld. She was inviting in all that might present itself to her in the darkness of night and the pale light of morning. She was ready to have more of her secrets revealed. She had discovered so much about herself, but still knew there was always another, deeper layer. And she was eager to see what was beneath.

As she wrote in her journal, no light entered the room. Hannah's hand passed over each page, her fingers nimbly guiding her pen, her eyes closed. It was as if she was channeling a message, auto-writing the wisdom from beyond. She knew there was little time to spare, and she couldn't mince words or concern herself with typos or phrasing. All that mattered was that she captured the world she had just been in and the messages it held. Therein lay all she needed to know.

CHAPTER SIXTEEN

THE GARDEN

Hannah went to check on Jezebelle and found the stain spreading across all of her fingers, down her knuckles and branching out into her hands with dark purple veins.

Hannah sat in reflection, her mind once again tracing the details of what happened the night they opened the 999 portal. Each one of them had held the mirror up to themselves. But what had everyone seen? Hannah knew what she had seen, although she hadn't shared it with anyone. She had seen all the expectations, negative projections, guilt, fear, and shame placed by others. She saw her own self-sabotage. Yes, it may have come from outside her, but she had consumed it like a large meal on an empty stomach, thinking she needed it, thinking they must be right. Believing till it became real. That internalization had become reality, had become truth, and once it did, the repetition of those discouraging words and avoidant behaviors simply reinforced what was already ingrained, already entrenched in her cells.

She had allowed others to infiltrate her once optimistic and peaceful mind, to soil her garden of plentiful flowers sprouting from seeds toward the glowing sun, confident with only the wind on their stems and earth beneath them. After her parents died, a dark cloud had emerged over her peaceful garden, breaking open and spitting dark and heavy globs of oily doubt and darkness, soiling the color the flowers once had, bending their leaves, weighing them down with the weight and heaviness of negativity.

This dark shadow lay underneath a layer of apparent assuredness. It had doubt, fear, and worst of all, it passed judgment. In fact, judgment was really what had catalyzed her insecurity to begin with. But was it her own self-judgment or the judgment of others? Or was other's judgment something she had internalized, letting it form the foundations of her own reasoning?

It most likely had not been her shadow to begin with, but over time she had merged with it as it soaked into the soil. Her garden was thirsty and cracked from lack of moisture, stems thin and weak without nourishment. A fertilizer of negativity had become the regular lifeblood of her garden. Whenever Hannah looked back at her life, she knew that some days she had been totally content, but then she encountered the outside world. That was when she would start picking herself apart like a hungry raven pecking at crumbs on the ground. Her thoughts would spiral into negativity around what she hadn't done or accomplished yet.

She still sometimes wondered if she could even make it on her own? After all, she had come to live at the manor because she had been unceremoniously relieved of her job as a pianist at the Midnight Lounge in her hometown. Her life back in Morningside had been fun at times, but she had struggled. She'd escaped that struggle by coming to Maple Hollow, and initially, as she built her life with her aunt, her new work filled her with a wholeness she had never experienced before.

But now that some time had passed, the creeping doubt about her own worth had returned. Yes, she knew she now had a calling, and yes, she knew she was helping others and there was more to do, but she couldn't help feel that it wasn't enough, that the goal posts were always moving further and further away from her. But was her mind doing this to her? The hamster wheel of doubt she had finally rolled off of when she came into her power on the island was starting to pick up speed again, taking her in a new direction of doubt. She knew it was up to her to stop it before it gained speed.

Chapter Seventeen

THE ECLIPSE

Hannah made her way down to the kitchen where Wendy was standing over the stove.

"Good morning, can I get you something, Hannah?" Wendy asked pleasantly.

"I'm fine, I'll just grab something quick since I'm on my way to town," Hannah said, opening the freezer to snatch a box of waffles, popping one in the toaster.

"What are you making?" she asked to pass the time while it heated.

"I'm putting together another potion for Jezebelle. I hope you don't mind me taking over the kitchen," Wendy probed. "I know it was supposed to be just for the dinner. But I feel responsible for her and can't see myself leaving her here, especially while she's so sick."

"Oh, not at all," Hannah said reassuringly. "I don't really cook, so you can stay as long as you like if it were up to me!" Her waffle popped up in the toaster, she flipped it onto a plate, doused it with a hearty drizzle of sweet maple syrup and quickly devoured it.

"Oh good, I'm glad to hear that. I'm happiest when I'm cooking," Wendy smiled, turning back toward the stove contently.

Hannah hopped on her bike and headed toward Maple Moon to feed Merlin and Milu.

Once she arrived, she doled out their food and decided to relax on the couch while they were eating. She liked to give them plenty of visiting time, but she also was feeling a bit sleepy after having woken up so early. Her eyes were drawn to a postcard on Morgan's coffee table from July advertising the solar eclipse. Being that it was a historic event, in fact the longest total solar eclipse of the century, Morgan had invited her to watch it with her at Maple Moon. The totality period had lasted nearly six minutes. The news had reported that another eclipse of that length would not occur for another hundred years. Hannah's eyelids became heavy as she slumped into the cushions and drifted off to sleep.

***

The sky was beginning to darken in a sort of pre-twilight. The black lamps that lined the streets were illuminated with a warm orange glow. All the bushes nestled around the small shops were a beautiful autumn gold, orange, and red, and the shop windows were lit up from the inside. And as Hannah approached Maple Moon, it seemed to glisten like a star. When she opened the glass door, a tiny bell rang above her, announcing her arrival. She was immediately immersed in the glowing mystical interior.

"Hannah, my dear, come in, come in! You are just in time for the eclipse," Morgan said as she floated toward her from the back of the store. She was holding a large candle in one hand and a book in the other.

"Morgan, so good to see you!" Hannah embraced Morgan in a hug.

"Always," Morgan replied. "Now come sit," she said. "We have a few minutes before it starts." She patted the back of a comfortable chair next to a small table. "I'll get some tea," she said as she disappeared behind the curtain in the back. She appeared again holding an elegant pot with a sparkly moon emblem. The room was aglow with a purple-blue hue and soft candlelight. Merlin followed closely at Morgan's heels. Hannah reached down to pat Merlin's head as he pranced by.

"There you go, my dear." Morgan poured the hot liquid between the small cups.

A tall lantern sat in the middle of the table. The flame inside flickered and glowed. White steam rose from both of the cups, rising up to touch each woman's nose as they bent over to inhale the herbal aroma.

"Dreams again?" Morgan asked, extending her hand across the table to Hannah.

"Actually, yes, you read my mind," Hannah said.

"Go on, dear," Morgan said.

"Why do we dream? What purpose do they serve in our lives?"

"Ah, I see, so many good questions, yes." Morgan leaned back and ran her fingers across the bookshelf behind her. "As you know, my dear, dreams exist in our inner realm. What might appear as the 'real world' to others is simply a collective illusion we all agree to stamp as reality, when in fact there is so much more. In our inner realm, we can go beyond this world into the next. We may live what appear to be alternate lives, see the past, see the future, but of course all of these concepts rely on linear time to even be conceived. Dreams are beyond space and time. They are not bound by the limitations of the earthly realm. In our minds, we have the ability to remember who we were before we came here, and what we still are, at a higher level. Our dreams tell us stories. Like books in a library, they show us things to teach us, to comfort us, to guide us."

"But how can we understand them? I've tried to look up different parts of my dream, but I can never seem to really get an answer that resonates with me. It's like the answers never relate to me."

Morgan rose from her chair and walked across the room to a large bookshelf. On each level of the shelf were small bowls, each one filled with crystals and gemstones of different colors and sizes. "Never look outside yourself for answers that lie within. One of the secrets of Maple Hollow is our traditions, and this book holds one of those secrets." She passed a worn and ancient book across the table toward Hannah. It wasn't a large or thick book like the *Grimoire de Skye*, but it did look just as old, likely having crossed the seas with the original founders of the island many moons ago. The words *Dream Awakening* were carved into the cover, and the letters were highlighted with stars and moons.

"What is it?" Hannah said as she pulled it closer to her, running her fingers across the unusual engravings on the cover.

***

Hannah suddenly awoke, Merlin and Milu were rapidly chasing each other around the apartment and scampering up on the couch, just missing her legs with their claws. She realized she had just seen Morgan in her dream. That she had gone back to the day of the eclipse. But even more than that, she realized Morgan was trying to tell her something. To look to her dreams for answers. That perhaps the nature of dreams was similar to the nature of mirrors. That she was leading her to awaken to the wisdom of her dreams to see beyond the mirror. She had actually given her that same book in real life. She had to go find it, perhaps it held the answers she'd been looking for all this time.

CHAPTER EIGHTEEN

THE TOWER

Hannah finished cleaning up the cat's dishes and headed back to the manor. She checked on Jezebelle once more, and a sick feeling in the pit of her stomach emerged when she realized the stain had spread to fill Jezebelle's palms with dark lines and cover the backs of her hands. But before she could dwell on it any further, Midnight came running through the room and out into the hallway.

Hannah followed his quick pattering paws. She felt he wanted to show her something and she was more than willing to oblige. But the faster she walked, the faster Midnight scurried. The manor itself had so many levels: the basement, which included the secret room under the library; the main floor, with the library, parlor, kitchen, and great hall; and the many bedrooms along the hallway at the top of the grand staircase. There was a third level above that, nearing the peak of the house, where the ceilings were slanted but still tall. Yet what Hannah had never noticed, even from the outside, was that there was yet another, and apparently secret, level above that.

She found herself standing before a doorway that was slightly ajar. She gently pushed it open, the hinges releasing a loud creak. "Midnight, wait!" she yelled, as he scampered up the stairs leading into one of the turrets of the manor. There were four turrets to the manor, one on each corner, standing like guideposts calling in the four elements. They bookmarked the center of energy the manor held. Each one was slightly different, some looking over the pumpkin patch and others out to the sea.

Midnight stopped abruptly in front of an armoire.

"Did you find what you're looking for?" Hannah asked, catching her breath. "Is this what you've been going on about? An armoire?" she asked in disbelief. Why had Midnight put her to a chase all that way just to stop in front of a piece of furniture?

It was a lovely armoire, after all, and having been instructed to notice, Hannah took a moment to admire it. It was nearly as tall as she was, with beautiful carvings on the surface. A massive maple tree was etched in the center, split down the middle by the break in the doors and the handles on each side. Across the whole surface ran a vast network of vines, interconnecting like the Celtic knotwork she had seen so often throughout the manor. The armoire must be ancient, she decided. She carefully pulled on one of the ornate handles.

It didn't budge. "It's locked, of course," she said, delivering the disappointing news to Midnight.

Midnight sat flapping his tail, unphased, blinking his eyes as if to say, "Try something else, then."

Hannah looked about the room. This most certainly was something that required a key. And the manor was full of keys, particularly in the great hall, which had a grand wall full of keys of all shapes and sizes. But

Hannah also remembered when her aunt had told her she *was* the key. She had been the key to the pumpkin patch, the key to defeating the Dream Haunters, the key to unlocking her own powers. She had learned this lesson well.

A flash of warm remembrance came over her when she remembered the key Jewelia had gifted her that fateful day after they defeated the Dream Haunters. She had placed the chain around Hannah's neck and invited her to come live at the manor. Hannah looked down now at the key hanging from the sparkly silver chain. She reached for the clasp, unhooking it from her neck, and then slowly placed the key into the lock on the armoire.

As she gently pressed it into the hole, attempting to turn it right, she felt the lock give and heard a distinctive clicking sound that could only mean this was a match. The lock gave way and popped open. Hannah slowly opened the armoire door.

There were no drawers inside, just a full-length mirror at the back. As she creaked open both doors, one in each hand, initially all she saw was darkness. Midnight immediately ran in.

"Midnight, wait!" Hannah said once again, but Midnight disappeared into the darkness.

He was small, but not so small to be lost in an armoire, or was he?

She peeked her head inside and realized it wasn't an armoire at all. As she looked into the mirror, she saw a reflection that was actually another passageway. Raising her foot off the ground, she took her first step inside.

CHAPTER NINETEEN

THE ARMOIRE

As she stepped into the armoire, Hannah grabbed her phone from her pocket and turned on the flashlight. In front of her was a narrow hallway. She started down it, hoping to find Midnight.

"Midnight, wait for me," she whispered.

When she got to the end, she realized she'd reached a turret, with a spiral staircase leading up. She could see the passing swish of Midnight's tail leading her further, so she made her way up the stairway.

When she finally reached the top, she saw that there were tiny windows all around a circular room. She drew closer to look out at a fantastical view of the sea. From this height, it was quite breathtaking. "What a view!" Hannah exclaimed as she took in the sights.

Midnight was sitting in one of the windows, an apparent smile on his face as if to say, "This is what I was trying to show you."

"I would have never known this was here," Hannah told him. "Aunt Jewelia must have wanted me to find this. It must be why she gave me this key, out of all the hundreds of keys there were to choose from. But still, why? What am I supposed to discover in this secret tower?"

She stood for a moment longer, looking out the window at the vast clumps of forest that surrounded the manor. The turret soared high above the greenhouse, and she could see the path to the icehouse in the woods. Her eyes searched the trees for any sign of Morgan. Then she turned from the window and realized that the back side of the circular room was now what could only be described as an optical illusion. It was as if the walls, floor, and ceiling were covered with mirrors.

She blinked in confusion. She was staring straight into a multi-layered reflection that replicated itself into an infinite horizon.

She suddenly heard Morgan's words echo in her mind, *"So much of what we need to know is hiding in plain sight."*

"Midnight?" she said cautiously.

Hannah turned once more toward the windows, then back toward the door. Her heart dropped in her chest. This time, as she stared at the exit, Midnight stood in the doorway, and on either side were bare walls. There were no longer any mirrors in the circular room.

"What's going on, Midnight?" Hannah demanded. "Why did you bring me up here? Whose room is this?"

The cat stood up from his comfortable sitting position and ran down the spiral stairway.

"Wait!" Hannah ran after him, leaving behind the empty room.

When she made it back down the spiral staircase and through the hallway, she saw Midnight sitting, waiting for her. She walked through the armoire, re-entering the room she had left, and closing the armoire doors behind her.

"What was that?" she asked in disbelief, looking at Midnight as she turned the key to lock the doors once more. She knew she had to go talk to Jewelia right away. After all, she had given her the key that unlocked the armoire.

She made it down from the top floors of the manor to the bedroom level and walked toward Jewelia's room as fast as she could. But when she arrived, Jewelia's bed was made and she was nowhere to be found in the room. Hannah decided to head downstairs, figuring Jewelia must be in the kitchen getting dinner.

She found Jewelia sitting with tea in the kitchen, nose down in a book. "I found a room in one of the turrets! Midnight led me there," Hannah said, but Jewelia didn't look up.

"I'm sorry, what, love?" she said, a distracted expression on her face.

"The turret. There's a room in it,"

"Yes, of course. That is why I gave you the key. I knew you would find it when the time was right." Jewelia smiled.

"It was full of mirrors," Hannah continued not sure how to explain the sudden appearance and disappearance.

"That's quite common around here," Jewelia said coyly.

"I mean, the whole room was a mirror, for a moment," Hannah stammered, still not quite explaining.

"That room is very special, my love. It is a portal. To some it appears empty, to others...full. It can transport you to places as well as transport things to you. Whatever the universe needs you to see can appear in that room."

Hannah considered what Jewelia was suggesting. "So, it's different for everyone?"

"Exactly. You can't show me because it won't show *me* the same thing as you. We all need to see things at our own speed, in our own time. The universe picks how it chooses to show us, in a way that is unique to us."

Hannah thought back to her dream where she was saying, *"Show me."* Perhaps she had conjured up the vision the room showed her, but why?

CHAPTER TWENTY

THE PATH

Despite all that had happened over the past few days, Hannah knew she needed to take a respite. She couldn't keep going at this pace if she hoped to locate Morgan and cure Jezebelle. Sometimes the giant light bulbs only appeared once she stepped back and took a break from her intense vexing.

It was a Friday, and Hannah was scheduled to play piano at the Whispering Whiskers Lounge until ten. Shortly after moving to the island, she had found a nice, little cat café that doubled as a piano bar at night, where she could once again play in public. The lounge was owned by twin sisters, Varlina and Delvina. By day, Varlina ran the bakery and café, and at night Delvina transformed the space into a sultry wine bar. But at all times, it was filled with cats.

Hannah was happy not to have to give up playing the piano for guests and patrons, which she'd enjoyed so much at the Midnight Lounge. Providing enjoyment for others through her music always had a way of helping her. Whenever she was going through change, or feeling anxious, sad, or lost, music had the power to uplift her soul and change her vibration for the better.

She instinctively knew this was also the reason why people liked to listen to her play. And it was not just a performance. When she shared music with others, it created a magick she could scarcely describe, one she knew she could not live without.

Ashlin had texted her that morning about getting together to compare notes, so she'd told her to stop by the lounge later that night.

She was just finishing her final song when she saw Ashlin come through the front door. Hannah was tired, but the crowd had seemed to have enjoyed her music nevertheless, and seeing Ashlin picked up her spirits.

"Hey, how are you?" Ashlin said as she approached, reaching out to hug Hannah. "And who's this?" she asked, pointing at the large tortoiseshell tabby loafing on top of the piano and absorbing the vibrations.

"This is Nutmeg," said Hannah. "She loves when I play. She always comes and sits here for my shows." She caressed the cat's ears and Nutmeg pressed her head harder into her fingers, as if to ask for more.

Then Hannah stood up. "Let's go get a drink. We need to talk." They retreated to a small table in the corner and sat sipping cold cocktails in the candlelight. "I don't have any updates on Morgan's whereabouts," Hannah said defeatedly as she sat down. "And Jezebelle's condition is getting worse every day. It's spread to cover all of her hands now. I fear we're running out of time."

Ashlin offered Hannah a look of condolence and reached out her hand. "I know it doesn't all make sense right now, but I'm sure there's an explanation for everything that's happening." She paused as her gaze wandered. "Look, the other night when you came to the library, I know you saw me," Ashlin remarked, but in a comforting not accusatory tone.

Hannah wasn't sure what to say. She'd been mulling over seeing Ashlin levitating amongst the books. "Well, yes…I did," she replied cautiously.

"That's what I wanted to talk to you about," Ashlin said, picking up her cocktail and twirling around the straw. "Just like you and your aunt, my family line has a legacy as well."

"Old Man Adams told me you were the keeper of wisdom," Hannah acknowledged, "and Jewelia said it was your family's legacy. But what exactly can you do?"

"Where other people have to use their eyes to read books, we communicate with them in a different way," Ashlin began. "It's more like a dance, where their information translates to us on an energetic level without needing to read. This is why my family are the holders of the knowledge. We can access information more quickly than people without our powers. It gives us a philosophic edge, I guess."

Hannah's eyes widened at her friend's revelation. "So…you're saying you can absorb the information without reading, somehow? That's amazing! I wish I had that power!"

"In a way, yes," Ashlin confirmed. "The messages contained within the book by the author are like a message in a bottle. When the bottle opens, we receive that message directly from the writer, not from the book. But there's more."

Hannah leaned in. She was waiting for Ashlin to explain not only how she was absorbing the information, but how she was levitating.

"When we communicate with the books, our body lifts to a higher plane to receive the information. It's essentially levitating, since the state we move into raises our vibration and thereby our physical body."

"Ah, yes," Hannah said, relieved at the confirmation of what her eyes had witnessed. "I'm sorry I didn't say anything about it. I felt embarrassed I had barged in."

"No, I'm sorry I didn't say anything to you yesterday. It must have come as quite a shock."

"Well, I've come to expect the unexpected in Maple Hollow," Hannah said, putting her hand over Ashlin's. The comforting warmth transferring her understanding across the table.

In fact, she found solace in Ashlin's revelation. Knowing that she wasn't the only one attempting to integrate her powers made her feel less alone. She could understand why Ashlin was quiet about it. It piqued Hannah's curiosity and she wanted to know more.

"Of course, now I'm wondering if I can do it too," she said. "I have so many books I want to read and so little time to read them."

"Since your family is tied to this island, it's possible you have the ability, at least to some extent," Ashlin said, leaning back in her chair. "Next time you go to your library, instead of trying to read the book, try to listen to the book and see what happens."

"I'm definitely going to do this. I'm excited to try," Hannah said as she sipped the last of her drink. Maybe if she could access the secrets of the library this way, she could learn what had happened to Jezebelle and Morgan.

When Hannah returned to the manor, she went straight to the library. It was late and the wind whipped at the windows as she sat bathed in candlelight with a stack of books around her.

She recalled what Ashlin had told her, and knew she should not open the books. Instead, she opened her mind. She worked on leading her mind toward a state that was similar to her dreamwork, a meditative state that allowed her to pass into the otherworld while still being mindful of her physical one. But she heard nothing...no vision, no whisper, no wisdom from the beyond.

Frustrated, Hannah began to think about Morgan. The day of the eclipse last summer, Morgan had asked her if she ever worked with stones. *"A wonderful addition to your practice,"* she'd said. *"Each one has its own spirit, its own benefits."*

Then Morgan gave her a small purple stone, an amethyst. She had explained that amethysts were semi-precious stones, part of the quartz family, and could help facilitate deep sleep. But they could also activate intuitive senses, allowing one to harness the spiritual wisdom of dreams by activating the third eye chakra. Morgan told Hannah to place the amethyst under her pillow when she went to sleep. She also said that Hannah was welcome to help herself to any of the stones at Maple Moon, her compliments.

Hannah had been intrigued to hear about the power of stones; she never knew they could be used for anything more than jewelry. This conversation had made her curious about what benefits or qualities other stones held. She did discover that putting the amethyst under her pillow helped with intensifying and focusing the whispers of her dreams. But now she wondered if it could help her learn how to open her mind and hear the books.

She quickly went upstairs to get ready for bed. After retrieving the stone from her bedside table, Hannah placed the amethyst under her pillow and fell into a deep dream.

***

She found herself standing on the dock at the manor. She could clearly see the full moon reflecting upon the sea. Its oversized orb practically filled the horizon. The water glistened with its milky reflection. At first, she was alone, and then her aunt was at her side.

Jewelia's voice echoed in Hannah's mind as she showed her what was ahead. The subtle waves in the water began to calm and the surface of the ocean became still, like glass, translucent and serene, transforming into an invisible mirror.

Without words, Jewelia raised her hand, motioning to the water. Hannah understood she was inviting her to move forward. She raised her right foot and placed it gently into the sea. To her surprise, it did not plunge in; her skin did not get wet and the water did not rise around her foot. Instead, the water stood firm, supporting her as if she were on land. Hannah leaned all of her weight on her foot and felt supported from beneath. She placed her left foot onto the surface as well.

She felt a sense of trust and ease come over her. It was as if the universe was telling her it was time to surrender, to become one with something greater than herself. There was a time when she had feared that drowning, dilution, and invisibility might be the result of merging with the vastness of the unknown. But now, as she stepped away from the solid land she'd always known, she gave herself over to the fluidity.

As she did, she could see a new path laid out before her in the water. Her aunt encouraged her to continue. Hannah walked further away from shore and down the moonlit path of the mirror walk. She began to see that her past perceptions about what would happen once she stepped off the land were all illusions. She had convinced herself that she knew the laws of nature, the ways of the world, what was and what was not. Yet by taking the plunge, embarking on this new path, the mirror had shown her it was not as she had expected, that she would not lose herself, that she had nothing to fear. The mirror walk was there to support her, inviting her in, illuminating her path, showing her the way. It was a mirror in a dream, a dream mirror.

Chapter Twenty-One

THE SKYE MIRROR

September 12, 2009

It was early morning when Hannah woke up. She grabbed her dream journal and started to write down the whole dream about the mirror walk. But she didn't have time to reflect on it further, since she'd awoken with an idea in her mind and had to see it through right away. Although she'd experimented with the amethyst to help her with her dreams, she realized that she had never followed through on her intention to study other stones and *their* properties. Maybe there was a different stone that could help Jezebelle heal. Or maybe there was one that could help her find Morgan.

She scurried out of her bedroom and over to the room where Jezebelle was. She went straight for her hand. To Hannah's shock, the stain now had spread past Jezebelle's wrist. Her entire hand was a dark purple, filled with what looked like the dark roots of a tree or the branches of a lightning bolt. Was she losing her circulation? Had she been infected by something? Or was something sinister slowing overtaking her? The further the stain spread, the more worried Hannah became.

She decided she'd get her exercise in with her errand. Grabbing an apple for the road, she ran outside, hopped on her bike, and started down the long road to town. A low fog that had crept in from the ocean was spreading across the pavement. The wisps intermingled with the spinning speed of her bike wheels as she whisked through the mist.

When she entered Morgan's shop, she went straight to the crystal bookshelf and gazed at the array of stones. "But which one?" she wondered out loud. Then heard the echoes of Morgan: *"You will discover in time."*

In her mind, she asked to be guided to the stone that would most help Jezebelle. She held her hands over the small bowls, like she had seen Morgan do in the past. Perhaps she had to feel into this, using her mind's eye. As her fingers passed over the bowls, they began to tingle. She became aware immediately which stone she should pick.

She reached out to grab a black, shiny, round stone. Then she picked up the sign next to it that read: *Hematite, a stone of the mind, can remove self-limiting beliefs. It also can strengthen the spiritual connection to other realms while providing safety and security.*

"I guess this is it!" Hannah announced to the hungry cats, placing it in her pocket. She fed Milu and Merlin, taking care to spend time and play with each one, then made her way downstairs and locked up the shop.

On the way back to the manor, she stopped to walk along the shore. She always liked to go down to the water. There was something so freeing about being near it...its fluidity, its freeness, its lack of structure. It had no bounds; it could be fierce as fire or as gentle as a breeze. It could destroy or heal. It was everything all at once. As she watched the waves crash upon the rocks, she knew the sea was part of her and that she must always be near it. It was showing her a way, like a light in the darkness. *Move*, it told her, *move your body like this*, as if it were showing her how to release the rigidity of her soul, the shell she'd created around herself that held her in place. Sometimes she was comforted by that shell, since it shielded her from the harsh world outside, but other times she realized this protection was in fact her prison.

Without Madame Morgan to consult about these things, Hannah knew she needed to rely on her own resources to discover how to stop the Illusionix. Jewelia had taught her a lot about mirror magick, but Hannah couldn't shake the nagging feeling that she was missing something about how to defeat the dark forces she now faced. She thought about the hidden room in the turret, the overhead view of the grounds, and the fantastical, mysterious mirrors.

That evening, while taking an after-dinner walk on the grounds, she noticed a large convex mirror that was attached to the exterior of the manor. She hadn't really noticed it before, nor realized that it was in fact a mirror. Its apparent utilitarian purpose had let it pass uninventoried in her assessments.

As she stared up at the mirror, she thought of the dragonfly she'd seen the other day at the shore. She realized the viewpoint of the mirror was rather like a dragonfly's. The mirror would reflect not just a straight-ahead image but an almost full 360-degree view. Perhaps this was the mirror she needed to do the trick.

Hannah had never really put it all together until now. Her aunt had disappeared during a large storm; Old Man Adams had told her as much that day in the foyer while Jewelia was still missing. And the night they opened the 999 portal, when Morgan disappeared and Jezebelle fell into her frozen state, that too had happened during a thunder and lightning storm. Were storms a metaphysical passageway? A transitional key between places and stages of existence? In her dream-world, she had asked her guides to show her what could not be seen. Morgan had told her it was hiding in plain sight. Jewelia had shown her in her dream that she could walk on water. She was going to harness the lightning and summon the Illusionix.

She walked quickly to Old Man Adams' cabin and knocked on the door.

"Well, hello, little lady," Adams said with a glint of joy in his eyes when he saw Hannah at the door. "There's a storm headed this way. Come on in," he said, stepping aside from the door to let her in.

"I actually need your help with something at the manor. Can you grab a tall ladder?" Hannah asked.

"Of course." He looked mildly surprised. "Where do you need it?"

"On the far side of the manor, there's a mirror on an outside corner...I need to take it down," she said.

"You got it, let's go." He closed the cabin door behind him and they headed back to the manor, carrying the ladder between them.

Once they retrieved the mirror, they returned to the cabin. "This storm is looking to be a bad one. We better batten down the hatches with some tea and hearty scones," he proclaimed.

Hannah followed him in, deep in thought. He invited her to sit with him and brought out a plate piled high with maple -frosted scones and a small teapot with mugs. As they relaxed in the cozy armchairs facing his small fireplace, Hannah waited and watched the barometer on the wall. Its red liquid overflowing was her signal that a storm was near.

She was now beginning to wonder if her parent's accident had happened during a storm. And the larger question loomed in her mind as to whether she could enchant the storm to reverse their fate. But there was no time to think about that. She had to harness the lightning before the storm rolled past.

As the dark clouds circled above the cabin, and the smell of the air wafting in from a nearby window sweetened, she knew in her soul the storm was close. She saw the bright flashes of lightning in the distance. The thunder began to roll in, quickening her heart.

"Thanks, I've got to go," she said, jumping up from the armchair. She ran out of the confines of the cabin toward the place where it all began, the pumpkin patch. The vines welcomed her as she stood among them, beginning to wrap around her ankles in greeting. She knew that their protective, grounding energy would be needed for this task, and obliged. Her dark cloak whirled around her as she stood holding the large domed mirror out in front of her body. She watched the storm overhead, through the reflection of the glass.

"*Taispeáin Dom an Tintreach,*" The words dropped from her mouth like darts into the air.

Without warning, an immense bolt of lightning struck the mirror. It was a direct hit, as if magnetized to the mirror, setting off a crack and a slam that took the wind out of her. An instantaneous flame singed the edges of her hood. Hannah's body blew backward, and she dropped the mirror as she fell hard to the ground.

Once she came to, the storm had passed and Jewelia was standing over her, helping her up. "Hannah! My love, what happened? Are you okay?"

Hannah looked to the ground and she saw the mirror, the glass cracked. "Did it work? Did I capture the lightning?" she asked in a daze.

"You created a Skye Mirror," Jewelia said, adjusting Hannah's cloak and patting down her hair. "Pure genius, that was," she said proudly.

"What do you mean, a Skye Mirror?"

"Skye mirrors are the link between the cosmos and our physical world. They can be created many ways. As part of our legacy, we can enchant them to harness the elements of nature. When we wield them, we can call upon them to aid us. But the conditions must be right."

"What are the conditions?" Hannah asked.

"It must be between a full moon and a new moon," Jewelia replied.

Hannah looked up at the sky. "The moon is in the last quarter. What other conditions?"

"Let's just say it requires the attainment of a certain level of spiritual awakening. One must somewhat relinquish their physical form to be able to merge with the subatomic level of particles outside of it. It is an energetic dance with nature." Jewelia picked up the mirror and handed it to Hannah.

Hannah knew in her soul she had passed through a threshold. That she had achieved what Jewelia explained and that now she could harness the elements to capture the Illusionix. "Let's get inside and get some tea. It's late and you need rest after that." She led the way back into the manor. Hannah's eyes watched the skies as they walked, the wheels of her mind turning faster.

Chapter Twenty-Two

THE COMMUNING

Hannah went straight to the bookshelf in her room and pulled out the *Dream Awakening* book Morgan had given her. She'd meant to read it nearly every day since she'd laid eyes on it, but the time had somehow escaped her. She was ready to try Ashlin's technique again, even though she didn't quite know where to start.

She sat cross-legged on her bed, the book in front of her, and closed her eyes. She placed her hands on the book, much like she would on a pumpkin. Maybe she had to make a physical connection with the book for it to connect with her mind. She waited in silence, trying to squelch any impatience that arose within her. She also tried to hold a blank space in her mind, one that could be filled by the book's wisdom.

Her right ear began to ring. She didn't move a muscle. She knew this could be a sign that the messages were about to begin, and she was ready to listen.

In her mind's eye, a movie began to play. She was the observer but also the creator. She tried not to force it, this co-creation of creativity. She wanted to receive and perceive. Hannah watched and waited; minutes passed as she lost herself in an altered world of words, symbols, and messages.

Her eyes snapped open and, to her surprise, the book on the bed was now on its back. Her hands were still on it, but she didn't remember turning it over. Had she read it with her mind? How would she know? It wasn't like people remembered every line of text they'd ever read, but there was usually a faint flicker of recognition, like when you started watching a movie seen years before. Something that tugs at the memory strings in a familiar yet in a mysterious way.

CHAPTER TWENTY-THREE

THE OWLS

That night, Hannah went to sleep with the amethyst and hematite stones underneath her pillow, and had a dream about two owls.

She found herself in a large arboretum, it was like the greenhouse at the manor, but colossally bigger. The daylight was blindingly bright inside, and it had a super high ceiling where the sun was shining in and she could see the white wispy clouds passing by against the bright blue sky above. She saw a small display area that appeared to be a mini koi pond with large fish swimming in it.

Just then a large white owl came swooping down. He landed and turned his head toward her. His face was flat with light gray feathers.

Hannah stared up at him in awe.

He reached out his right front claw and introduced himself. "Hello, I'm Filgrim," he said in a British accent.

"Hello," Hannah replied. They started to talk.

"We've been watching you for the past seven years," the owl said. "We should tell everybody so they are prepared for what's going to happen."

"Happen to who?" Hannah asked, confused. It felt like the owl was implying her time had come and that he was here to help in the transition. She had this innate sense that he was going to be informing people what was going to happen to *her*, although she wasn't sure what it was. He was revealing himself because it was time.

The scene suddenly shifted and Hannah found herself in her old neighborhood back in Morningside. It was one of those days when the sun was extremely bright, there were no clouds, and the sky was a deep cobalt blue. She stood on a sidewalk of a street lined with moderate-sized houses. She didn't recognize the houses, but she had a sense that she was standing outside one that was hers. A man, who was a neighbor, came out of one of the houses and approached her. On his head, was perched a peculiar large owl. But it wasn't Filgrim.

"Bow," the man said, which Hannah did obligingly. "There's someone I'd like you to meet," he continued, referring to the owl.

"Hello," the owl said in a friendly voice.

"Hello," Hannah replied as she put her hand out toward the trippy-looking owl. Her face was extremely ornate, and animated. It had multiple colorful layers that shifted and moved like a kaleidoscope. It was one of the most unique and beautiful things Hannah had ever seen.

The owl placed her claw on Hannah's hand.

"You might want to get more notebooks," the man instructed.

The owl spoke succinctly, as she stared into Hannah's eyes. "Now it is time, time to reveal ourselves, as you are ready for the next step." She flapped her wings and then wrapped them around her body.

Hannah gazed in wonder at the fantastical owl.

***

When she awoke, she lay still, trying not to move too much. She thought back to where she'd just been. It took a minute, but then she saw the carnivalesque rotation of the multi-colored, animated face of the owl. In a flash she remembered her dream, and her interaction with the man who introduced the owl. Was he a neighbor? And what had he told her?

She made herself pause, knowing those moments when she first woke up were a crucial time. The dream seemed hidden from her behind a cloak of consciousness. She tried not to move. Her body was heavy with the remnants of sleep. She tried to calm her mind and concentrate, yet remain in a serene state of flow uninterrupted by the outside world. Then the rest of the dream memory began to slowly reveal itself.

The image of the arboretum arose. And then from the ether, the image of the first owl materialized. She could see him in her mind's eye. He was probably a foot and a half tall. His eyes were black as night. His face was framed by a round circle of delicate fur that created a ring around it. The owl's presence felt significant and wise. He knew things and knew her. But what was he here to tell her about? What was going to happen and what was he going to tell her about it?

She grabbed for her dream journal but didn't want to break the brainwave flow she was still floating on. She held the small bound notebook in her hands, using her fingers to guide her pen. She couldn't see anyway in the darkness of the room, so she kept her eyes closed. She scribbled onto the page and as the paper cracked between her fingers, she remembered the last words of message from the dream: *"Get more notebooks!"* She smiled to herself. *I guess I should.*

When writing in her dream journal, sometimes she could only capture a few phrases as the dream escaped into the ether. But other times, it was as if she had just sat through a three-hour movie and the narrator's voice was still echoing in her head as her hand scrambled to transfer it all into words. This time, she didn't have much to write, but the images of the owls were distinct, fascinating, and clear. She knew there was more to it, but she still hadn't mastered the ability to figure it all out.

Midnight jumped onto the bed and began kneading about in an attempt to rouse Hannah from her resting place. She placed her pen inside the book, hooking it on the open page, and closed it halfway shut before placing it back on her nightstand.

The morning light was beginning to peek through the curtains and her body began to call for her to stretch and beckon in the blood flow necessary for her to begin her existence on the earthly plane once more. The spinning puzzle pieces of the second owl's colorful face faded fast away as she roused to enter her day.

As had become her routine every morning, Hannah went to check on Jezebelle again. Even from the hallway she could see that the purple stain had made it midway up Jezebelle's lower arm. It was creeping its way toward her elbow, nearly taking over her whole forearm. Wendy was sitting in an armchair nearby reading a book on healing agents. Hannah's wonderment from her dream quickly transitioned to worry and concern.

She walked downstairs to the kitchen, finding Jewelia at the stove making a warm pot of oatmeal.

"There you are, love," Aunt Jewelia said, turning with the spoon in her hand. The room smelled of warm spices, cinnamon, nutmeg, and allspice.

"It smells amazing in here!" Hannah remarked.

"I hoped the smell might wake Jezebelle. Come sit and have some breakfast," Jewelia offered, motioning her to the table.

"Aunt Jewelia," Hannah began, pulling out the chair and sitting down. "Remember when we talked about cats being spirit guides in our dreams? When you told me about Wixby?"

"Yes, of course, love."

"Well, I'm wondering if it's possible for other animals to be spirit guides, too."

"Yes, yes," Jewelia said, her eyes widening as she spooned large dollops of oatmeal into two bowls and passed one to Hannah. "Any animal, or insect for that matter, can be a spirit guide. In fact, anything on this earth can be, since it all has energy; from a gust of wind to the feather that floats on it. Any and all of it is here to commune with us, guide us, follow us through this experience here within it."

"That makes sense. I never really thought about it until recently, but I've been seeing more animals that talk in my dreams, just like Wixby."

"Ah. Well, now that you have awakened your awareness, they can all come in and communicate with you. That's wonderful." She took a deep gulp from her mug. "I have had so many over the years. I always find it comforting when I awake and discover I've met another."

"I'm always surprised what form they appear in," Hannah said, swiftly finishing off her oatmeal.

"Nature is filled with patterns...both patterns that we as humans follow, but also patterns that nature itself follows. The very fabric of our existence is a pattern. We have two eyes, two ears, two hands, for example, and when you look at a flower's petals you can see how concentric and perfect its patterns are. Have you ever noticed the patterns on a snail or a tortoise shell?"

"A tortoise?" Hannah perked up. "Funny that you say that. I had a dream a few years ago about a talking turtle!"

"Well, that's just what I'm talking about. You see, that tortoise was your spirit guide as well. They are here to help you fulfill your destiny. To guide you to where you are needed and support you along the way." She paused, a sense of frustration creeping across her face.

"I wish my guides would help me figure this out. I have tried something different nearly every day to find Morgan: spells, scrying, but nothing is working. What led you to create the Skye Mirror?" Jewelia asked in a curious tone.

"Funny you ask, but also a dream. Well, and a firefly. I figured out how to harness the lightning and I think this is how we can conquer the Illusionix. I'm going back to town. I'll stop by Morgan's and then go to see Ashlin."

"That sounds like a good plan. I will keep a close eye on Jezebelle once I finish up here. It appears her condition is worsening and our time may be short."

CHAPTER TWENTY-FOUR

THE TREES

SEPTEMBER 13, 2009

After breakfast, Hannah rode her bike downtown to Morgan's shop to feed Merlin and Milu. It was the least she could do for her old friend.

While she was sitting in Morgan's flat above Maple Moon, looking at her books once more, Merlin ran up to Hannah, stood on his back legs, and reached up to her elbow to tap her gently with his paw.

"What is it, Merlin?" Hannah asked.

She noticed that the sunrays gleaming through the windows were illuminating a different set of books, ones she had not noticed before as they were on a lower shelf. Merlin ran over to one and began tapping its spine with his paw.

"Are you trying to show me something?" Hannah asked as she grabbed the book. It featured a raised image of a large tree on its cover, the roots spreading around the back of the volume. She suddenly realized the similarity to the tree carving on the armoire doors in the turret. She ran her fingers across the roots and went to sit down in an armchair with the book.

The cover said *The Land of Brananagh*. She flipped through the pages, each chapter describing a different type of tree. She wondered if these trees were present in Maple Hollow. She came to one chapter called *The Imni*. Hannah's eyes and heart stopped on this one, although she wasn't sure why...until she started reading.

She read that the Imni was a magickal tree that wasn't always visible. It only appeared to those who needed to find it, but could heal all who laid eyes on it. This tree had particular powers: the power to release the finder from fear, doubt, and worry. It would only appear to one who was in need and consumed with their own vexation and anxiety. It existed in a different dimension. Whenever anyone's thoughts were focused on their doubts and worries, the tree could appear on the earthly plane. Fueled by the person's negative emotions, the tree had the ability to transmute this pain through its roots. It would pull all that darkness into the belly of the earth, sending positive energy back out that would illuminate its branches and leaves until the entire tree glowed like a luminous star.

As she continued to read, Hannah flipped to a page that had a black and white illustration, below which was inscribed:

The Imni of Maple Hollow.

This very special tree has the ability to relieve whomever finds it of all their worries, since worry is a projected illusion of a reality that does not exist yet, and may never exist. The present is a gift. Worry holds no purpose. It is purely an expression of fear that removes the present of its strength. Worry should be given away so we can experience the present more fully.

"So, the Imni is here in Maple Hollow?" she said out loud, her curiosity increasing even more. *Morgan must have known about it,* she thought. *Had she seen it? Used it? Who else knew about it?* Hannah was riveted by this story. There was something about it that she couldn't let go of, something that kept circling in her mind.

She suddenly remembered the rest of the conversation she'd had with Morgan the day of the eclipse. Morgan had said that each Healer of the Hollow had a different gift, which were all synergistically necessary together. *"We are messengers, visionaries, guides. We have the ability to see beyond what others can see. This is both a gift and a burden, but it is the burden we must bear to help the world evolve in the direction it must. It is a process of continual evolution that calls us all forth. We must heed the call and step into it."*

Morgan had shared with her that her own family's legacy was tied to the trees. Much like Hannah's connection to the pumpkin patch vines, Morgan's connection ran deep underground, with the trees and through their roots. It was, in fact, her ancestors who had charmed the trees of Maple Hollow to live year-round in the full glory of their true autumnal colors.

When they'd stepped outside to watch the eclipse, waiting inside a pocket of trees clustered around the back of the shop, Hannah had noticed that the birds were silent. It had become dark in the mini-forest. All the night flowers had begun to open their petals, ushering in the shadows. The crickets chirped and the spirits of the forest of the Hollow had begun their night dance. But it was not night at all.

As the shadow had slowly crept across the glowing hot orb of the sun, the heat gradually dissipated, leaving a cool trail of shadow in its wake.

Then a thick, eerie fog had begun to swirl around them. Hannah's attention had been drawn to a tree branch, upon which sat a large, white owl hooting from its perch. She watched the owl watching the skies, wise and still, turning her head left and right, intently listening to the tiny creatures crawling about in the brush. A new daytime dew coated the branches and leaves. Hannah had soaked in the night sounds of the owl, chirping crickets, and distant waves lapping on the shore.

She snapped out of her memory. *The fog! The trees!* Hannah realized she had to go discuss this with Ashlin. After all, Ashlin knew the island's history by heart.

She left Morgan's apartment and rode her bike toward the Maple Hollow Library. There had to be more information about the trees in there, and Ashlin could help her find it. She leaned her bike against the wall, which was starting to warm from the mid-morning sun.

As she crossed the threshold into the library, Ashlin looked up from the front desk with a warm smile. "Hannah, good morning! How is Jezebelle doing?"

"Same, I'm afraid," Hannah replied glumly.

"And Morgan, any word?" Ashlin raised an eyebrow hopefully.

"No," Hannah said with a sigh. "But I did discover something quite amazing."

"What's that?" Ashlin leaned in.

"I figured out how to use mirrors to harness lightning. Apparently, it's called a Skye Mirror. I think it's going to be the key to capturing the Illusionix."

"Fascinating," Ashlin smiled. "I found something too!" Ashlin grabbed a stack of books that was sitting next to her computer on the desk. "Have a seat," she said to Hannah, motioning to the closest patron desk.

They both sat down and Ashlin began to open all the books.

"We know there were a number of fruits served at the dinner that could have stained her nails," Ashlin began. "And Wendy confirmed that pomegranates or dragonfruit, could be the culprit. But I have a feeling there's something more." She pointed to one of the pages. "The elders of this land used to use the bark of the maple tree as a purple dye for clothing. And Jezebelle was in the woods. Is it possible the dye could have come from the trees?"

"I think that's possible," Hannah replied. "I've been going over to Morgan's to feed her cats, and while I've been there, I've been checking out her books. She has a lot that talk about the trees of the island. In fact, there's one in particular that definitely piqued my curiosity. It's about the myths of the trees."

"Oh, and?" Ashlin said eagerly, not wanting to interrupt but anxious to hear what Hannah had to say.

"Apparently there's a legend about a tree called the Imni tree. Have you heard of that one?"

"Let's look it up!" Ashlin bolted to her computer at the front desk. "How do you spell it?" she asked as she passed a sheet of paper to Hannah to write it down. "Here we go, the Imni tree. The legend states that the Imni tree exists between dimensions. It can be viewed on the physical plane, but only by those whose condition manifests it. The tree itself is a depository and transmuter of spiritual woes. It has the ability to consume and transform these woes through its own chemistry."

"So, do you think Jezebelle encountered or manifested the Imni tree?"

"But then..." Ashlin paused. "In that case she'd be cured, not sick, right? Isn't the point of the tree to heal?" She flipped the page. "Wait, there's something else here."

"What is it?" Hannah leaned over.

"It says the roots of the Imni tree are the channels by which all the negativity and woes are transferred to the earth for transmutation. The trickster known as the Illusionix, rules the underworld below the Imni tree, where they gather all the woes of the world. Originally, the fable said that the Illusionix agreed to take care of this negativity without using it against those that made deposits. But if the Illusionix is disturbed, they may break that vow, and use the darkness in nefarious ways against the depositer."

"That makes sense!" Hannah exclaimed. "Jezebelle must have done something to awaken the Illusionix. Does it say how to defeat it?"

"No, it doesn't. I'm going to have to think on this and do some more research. Look for any books on the Illusionix at Morgan's. I'll keep looking, too. There has to be a solution in one of these books."

"I meant to tell you, I had two dreams the other night about owls," Hannah said. "They spoke to me, just like you are now. I'm still trying to figure out what they mean."

"Hmm. As metaphors, owls can be about vision. They appear to remind us of intuition and illusions. They can see the full spectrum: the past, the future, and all aspects we cannot. The thousand-foot view, the 360-degree angle. Their perspective reminds us to not get caught up in just one way of looking at things. They implore our inner wisdom, our inner vision. They dispel the mystery of the unknown, but gift us with the eyes of wisdom which can see into the beyond. Perhaps we need to see beyond the obvious." She passed another book to Hannah.

Hannah's ears perked at mention of a 360-degree angle. She immediately thought of the convex mirror and the dragonfly. "It says here that owls are the messengers of the trees," Hannah said, pointing. "They live among them and are part of them, intrinsically. They deliver the wisdom to us in a way the trees cannot. They watch over the trees, in the cloak of darkness. They stand stoic in the dark of night, protecting the forest. Come to think of it, when the owl arrived that night at dinner, it must have been a messenger. I also saw an owl during the eclipse last summer," she added thoughtfully. "One of the ones in my dream was an amazingly beautiful owl. Her face was like an animated kaleidoscope; I'm not even sure how to explain it."

She continued to read aloud from the book:

Guides and messengers will present themselves to us. Each is unique and carries a message. We must maintain our openness, our curiosity, and our peaked awareness. This will allow the messages we are meant to receive to come in.

"Hmm. You might enjoy this book written in the 1800s by the inventor of the kaleidoscope." Ashlin stood up and walked over to a large bookshelf against the wall. She searched for a minute, then came back to the table with a large purple volume, passing it to Hannah.

Hannah flipped through the pages opening to one that read:

Kaleidoscopes are optical devices that use mirrors to create patterned geometric reflections. The word kaleidoscope draws its origin from several Greek words which roughly translates to "viewing a beautiful form." But how they work is really a function of position, incline, and angles. Essentially, perspective is everything. With the right illumination, the multiplication and combinations that can be seen are endless.

"Wow, I remember having one as a child. I always thought they were so fascinating, but I never knew how they worked. And mirrors?!" Hannah exclaimed, a veritable light bulb sparking over her head. "I totally forgot that kaleidoscopes use mirrors! Of course. It makes total sense. When we look into a mirror, the reflection we see is the light bouncing off the mirror emanating from our face. It is a light reflection. Such is the kaleidoscope as well. Viewed as a metaphor for life, kaleidoscopes could represent all the different perspectives we can have. Just when we look at something one way, when we slightly turn or twist, a new perspective emerges. The patterns are fluid, never fixed, if only we are willing to have a new perspective and be open to receive," she said, remembering her discussion with Jewelia about patterns. "It is a co-creation between our vision and the light. Together they awaken all the possibilities. The transformation we all can embody. I'm beginning to think that our entire reality is just a reflection. That it's an illusion reflected from our subconscious. It's like our whole world is a mirror box."

"Now you're onto something." Ashlin beamed.

"I'm going to head home and check on Jezebelle again. Jewelia and Wendy have been watching her. I'll call you if I find anything."

Hannah left the library, hopped on her bike, and headed back to the manor, leaves swirling behind her bike wheels like galaxies untold.

CHAPTER TWENTY-FIVE

THE MIRROR ATTACK

Hannah was sound asleep, but something jarred her from her slumber. Her eyes snapped open. She glanced at the clock and saw that it was the middle of the night. Her heart started pounding so loud in her ears, it nearly shut out all sound. Her breath was quick like she was midstream into running a marathon, her body preparing for fight. Adrenaline surged through her veins.

But what had woken her up? She'd heard something, almost like a snapping but more like a cracking.

As she tossed in bed, turning toward the door, she found herself looking across the room at the dresser. The rectangular mirror that sat above it had cracked in hundreds of places, spontaneously, leaving a fractured remnant of the once-smooth surface. The shards were mysteriously still in place, but the reflection of the room, enclosed within the gold maple leaf frame, was now splintered.

This was the mirror through which Hannah had first been able to read the mysterious letter her aunt had sent her, the one that told her for the first time not only about the Dream Haunters, but about the Skye family legacy and her role in saving it. The mirror had become special to her for that reason, and each morning and night she would look into the glass, remembering the moment she had passed the candle behind Jewelia's letter and the cryptic writing had swirled into meaning, revealing itself in a moment of clarity.

Distraught, as her fractured reflection could no longer find itself, Hannah didn't have time to think or wonder further. Her body was in full panic mode as she readied herself.

She ran out of her bedroom into the hallway. A strong wind blew through the open windows down one side, whisking her hair and nightgown as she ran toward Jewelia's room at the end of the hall.

As she went, each mirror hanging on the wall popped, cracked, and broke into tiny shards. Hannah's bare feet nearly avoided the glass falling on the ancient knotwork rugs as she ran, dancing between the tiny shards. When she reached the end, she pounded on her aunt's bedroom door.

"Jewelia," she yelled at the dark heavy wood that blocked her path.

Jewelia instantly sprang from bed and leapt toward the door. When she opened it, she saw Hannah standing in disarray, her nightgown torn and tattered from the shards of glass.

"What on earth has happened?" she implored, grabbing Hannah and pulling her into the room.

"The mirrors! They're all breaking!" Hannah yelled, out of breath and in a panic. "I woke up to the sound of my mirror cracking, and when I came to get you, all the mirrors in the hallway began to crack, too. It's like they were following me and I couldn't escape."

"The mirrors!" Aunt Jewelia's eyes grew wide, a look of grave concern crossing her face as she saw a thick fog rolling down the hallway behind Hannah. "They've come," she said, pulling Hannah inside and closing the door. She placed her hand on the doorknob as if she were waiting.

"Who, who's come?" Hannah asked in trepidation.

"Those mirrors are charmed. They have been by our family for hundreds of years. I have only seen one break a few times since I've lived here, and that was when I was very young. My mother had to replace a few, but I never knew how they broke. I guess I was too young to pay attention, and they likely protected me from it."

"Charmed...charmed how?" Hannah asked as she grabbed a pillow from Aunt Jewelia's bed, clutching it.

"You remember when I showed you how we use the mirrors? How we can train ourselves to look past our reflection and see beyond this world?"

"Yes," Hannah affirmed with anticipation.

"Mirrors are portals, unlike the pumpkins, they have two sides. One side we can see, and one we cannot. There are those in other dimensions who wish to cause us harm, and each mirror has a dark side that exists in their plane. It must be the Dark One of Phantasm. The Illusionix. Danger is upon us."

When her aunt said the word "danger," Hannah felt a sharp pain in her chest and her heart started pumping even harder. Her palms were sweating. She wasn't ready for this. What was happening?

"The fog!" she yelped, pointing at the door.

A low fog had begun to creep under the door, clinging to the hard floor and enveloping their ankles like a mossy swamp. Penetrating their mouths and nostrils, the fog began to make them both sputter and choke.

"It's here for Jezebelle!" Jewelia proclaimed. She threw open the door and plunged headfirst into the fog that now obscured their steps. They began to wince as their bare feet met the sharp shards on the rugs.

"*Ceo a Dhíbirt!*" Jewelia yelled down the hall, holding her arm out across Hannah to prevent her next step.

A loud boom of thunder rolled outside the manor, shaking its foundation.

"*Ar shiúl ceo ar shiúl!*" she shouted as the fog began to scurry under Jezebelle's door.

"I'm coming!" came a voice from the staircase. It was Old Man Adams, holding a broom and vigorously sweeping his way down the hall. "I heard the screams and came as fast as I could." He reached out to help Hannah and Jewelia across the glass as the fog quickly dissipated.

"Jezebelle!" Hannah yelled as she reached for Jezebelle's door. But no sooner had she opened it than she saw the fog disappearing into the mirror above the dresser next to Jezebelle's bed. It was the only mirror left unbroken.

"Are you all right?" Jewelia asked Jezebelle without thinking. But there was still no response. The depths of the woman's eyes seemed to spread into a deeper sorrow.

"Don't you worry. I'll get this cleaned up right away," Old Man Adams said reassuringly.

"Why is this mirror not broken?" Hannah asked, approaching the glass.

"Let's get some rest. We have more work to do tomorrow," Jewelia said, reaching out her hand for Hannah. Together they walked side by side into the darkness, through the shattered glass strewn across the hall.

Chapter Twenty-Six

THE LEAF

September 14, 2009

The sun was already high in the sky when Hannah awoke. Her neck was stiff. She wasn't sure if it was due to the pillow, or because Midnight had been sleeping curled up under her right arm all night, frightened by the attack. She didn't mind, of course. She'd loved when Mystera, her childhood cat, slept with her as a child. There was something so comforting about falling asleep syncing with the rhythm of their soft breath and their warm body. Cats had always been her cherished comfort, her companions in this world and the next.

When she'd met Wixby last year in the dreamworld, and then found out he actually used to be Jewelia's cat, prior to Midnight, it confirmed for her that, first, there was more to this reality than meets the eye. Second, dreams existed in a place beyond space and time. Thirdly, cats could bridge that space, just like she could.

Sometimes when Midnight would come sleep next to her, she felt intrinsically like he was both protecting her and accompanying her, ready for their expedition together through the otherworlds. Even cats needed to leave their bodies on a nightly basis, departing this world and visiting the next.

As she left the comfort of her bedroom and walked down the long drafty hallway toward the staircase, she walked past the empty mirror frames on the wall, their remnant broken shards reflecting the sunlight and grounds outside. The glimmering morning light accentuated the deep colors of the maple tree leaves glowing gold, orange, and red.

"Don't worry, little lady. I'm back to clean up the rest of this, now that it's daylight out," Old Man Adams said, appearing at the top of the stairs with a broom.

Hannah stopped in the doorway of Jezebelle's room and could see the stain was now past her elbow. "Oh Jezebelle," she whispered. "We're doing everything we can. We'll figure out how to fix this."

As she approached the top of the stairs, she could hear an assortment of loud noises coming from the kitchen. The scent of pumpkin spice wafted up to her nose, making her stomach growl and her feet move quickly down the stairs.

"Good morning, love," Aunt Jewelia said as she entered into the brightness of the kitchen. It was buzzing with the whistle of water rising to a boil for warm drinks, the hissing of that morning's food on the grill, the crackling of a glowing fire in the hearth, and the hot irons of the toaster browning the morning's bread. It made Hannah feel so comfortable and secure despite the unwelcome events of the night before.

"It smells wonderful in here," she said as she pulled out a chair at the large wooden table.

"It'll all be ready shortly," said Wendy. "Here's something to get you started." She placed a round plate in front of Hannah with a pumpkin muffin in the middle.

"Yum, my favorite." Hannah's mouth started to salivate in anticipation of what she was about to consume. She peeled the light wax lining off the muffin before raising it to her mouth and taking a bite, the sugary crumble leaving a mustache above her top lip.

"I'm glad. We always have plenty of pumpkins to cook with here in Maple Hollow," Jewelia said, a glow in her eye as she turned back to the stove.

As Hannah finished off the muffin, practically inhaling it, she thought about her pumpkin dream. The pumpkin patch was magickal, and she'd learned how to connect to it. But she had also faced dangers, especially when she first came to Maple Hollow. As she sipped her warm drink, she wondered what other dangers were ahead. They knew nothing about what the Illusionix could do, or what it wanted, or where it might appear next.

"Have you seen Jezebelle's arm?" she asked Jewelia. "It's getting so much worse."

"I did, and that is part of why I'm cooking this morning. Wendy has found some new ingredients we can add to her salve. This will hopefully slow the progression more effectively, if nothing else. The spell on Jezebelle is closer to its completion than ever before. And I fear the Illusionix can cross the threshold into the physical world whenever they want, as they did with the mirrors. Let's do some more research today when you get back from feeding the cats."

After Hannah returned from town, they went straight to the library. As Hannah perused the many books, she felt sorry that she couldn't read them all in this lifetime, and wished again that she could master Ashlin's power. But perhaps she'd made a little progress toward it the other night.

As she sat in the upholstered chair facing the large window, she heard a slight shifting noise behind her. It was Midnight, sliding through the cat door carved into the base of the door. She went back to reading and Midnight came and sat on her lap, enjoying the sun.

Hannah fished for a book on owls: *Owls: A Celtic Symbology Exploration*. She flipped through the pages and read:

The Celtic goddess Arianrhod was known as a shapeshifter, able to transform into the shape of an owl. She assumed this form so that she could travel through the cloak of night and in dreams. Serving as the messenger of the subconscious, she hails from the Aurora Borealis. A pillar of mystical knowledge and wisdom that exists in the darkness, she can reveal the shadow sides of our existence and deliver healing.

Hannah wondered if the owl at the 999 dinner, or the one at the eclipse, or the kaleidoscope one she had dreamed about could be Arianrhod. A Celtic goddess visitation to reveal her path? She continued to read.

Celtic mythology is filled with stories of owls. They serve as guideposts, ushers of mystery and wisdom. But some say they can also be messengers of death.

What if that meant Jezebelle wouldn't recover? Or Morgan was dead? While she was intrigued and comforted by the other aspects of the owl, she began to worry again about the fate of them both.

Suddenly Hannah remembered she was supposed to be researching a cure for Jezebelle. She promptly put the book on owls down and began pulling medicinal and curative texts from the shelves. She piled multiple books into small stacks and slowly flipped through the pages, book by book. But the subject matter was dry and her eyelids began to feel heavy. Before long, Hannah fell asleep into a dream.

***

A colorful Tiffany desk lamp perched atop a small wooden desk. Its glow shone like a spotlight on an abandoned coffee mug, now cold, its warm liquid having been consumed. It was dark green on the outside and white on the inside. Suddenly, Hannah's eyes lifted from the book she was reading to the mug as she saw two small eyes emerging near the rim. The eyes appeared as if they were on the end of a tiny snake rising out of the mug, but the body they were attached to was no bigger than the stem of a leaf. Then the full stem body stood up, preparing for introduction.

"Hello, I'm Leaf," he said. But he wasn't a leaf at all, just the stem of a leaf, which he promptly revealed by turning up the end of his stem, which was cut on a slant like with fresh-cut flowers.

It reminded Hannah of how, when her parents passed, there had been so many flowers sent to the house. Her grandmother had shown her how to trim the ends before putting them in vases, just like that. Except instead of the usual sadness she would feel when anything reminded her of that time, at this moment, she felt filled with wonder. While she was looking directly at Leaf, he blew magickal air out of the end of his stem. With fascination, Hannah put her hands up and could feel the air coming out. It was sparkly, with some tiny bubbles.

Then the dream shifted and she found herself at the shore. She stood with her feet embedded in a small cliff of sand. In front of her was a table, on top of which was a small sign. It appeared that the table was from a ceremony, as it was covered with a white tablecloth. There was a remembrance book, the kind where people sign their names and leave written memories. There was also a small electronic screen with a little button, which when she pushed it played a replay of a ceremony. Then the tablecloth slid off, and out popped Leaf. He began drawing a symbol with the end of his body onto an open page of the book.

***

When she woke up, she began to write down furiously what she had dreamt. Where had her dream taken place? It was on a shore of an island. But was it Maple Hollow or another island she'd never been to? Her feet were in the sand, but she also stood on a cliff. Even though it was small, Hannah knew what her associations were with cliffs. Her parents had met their fate off Lone Peak Cliff, and she'd had other dreams about cliffs.

Then she focused on remembering the objects. There was a small table with a white tablecloth that blew in the beachy breeze. She had the sense that maybe there had been a celebratory event. And the small sign reminded her of the kind you see in the forest that sit upon a trail or at crossroads, which help you find your way when you are on a path in the woods, so you don't get lost. Morgan had told her to watch the trees for signs. But she never figured out if Morgan meant actual signs or if she meant that the trees would act as indicators or guides. And there was the book for guests. A way to remember them by and mark that moment in time. Did the ceremony allude to the night of the 999 ritual?

What was Leaf drawing in the book? Was he a messenger? A messenger of the forest? She could faintly see in her mind the symbol he drew comprised of bold lines. But how could she find out what he was trying to show her?

Hannah knew instinctively that she was supposed to keep Leaf safe, that he would help her with his mystical element of air. He was of the forests of Maple Hollow. He was one of the many magickal creatures that lived there and could talk, just like Wixby. No matter how small, every animal, every insect had wisdom, a message, a power. She was only beginning to discover how much.

CHAPTER TWENTY-SEVEN

THE VORTEX

When Hannah awoke from her nap, she realized Jewelia was gone and the sun was lower in the sky. She'd spent most of the day in the library and needed some fresh air to shift her perspective.

As she was out walking in the woods behind the manor, she came upon a clearing. She didn't walk directly into it, and in fact might not have even noticed it, if it wasn't for the screech of an owl. Having just read about Arianrhod, this caught her attention. She gazed up and to the right, where her eyes were drawn beyond the path to a large circle outlined by stones on the ground. Inside was a spiral made by much smaller stones. All were placed in a particular pattern, curling into the center. She drew closer and walked to the opening.

It was there that buzzing sensation returned. It was what she had felt when she'd stepped off the ferry onto the island of Maple Hollow for the first time. When she'd passed from water to land and her feet had met the earth, a tingling sensation rose from her feet, up her legs, and into her body. And it was the same vibrating she felt when she connected with the pumpkin patch, the vines filling her with an earthly resonance unlike any other she'd ever felt.

Hannah suddenly remembered that there were books in the library at the manor about vortexes, and how Ashlin and Jewelia had told her the island was a vortex. Perhaps this circle of stones was some sort of concentration of that energy. The owl was leading her once more to discovery.

As her feet crossed the threshold of the stone labyrinth, the rhythmic hoot of the owl drew her along. Tiny forest creatures scurried beneath the leaves. She could intrinsically tell that she was meant to find this place of sanctuary. The interconnectedness of the island, the fog, the pumpkin patch vines, and her energy were merging into one force field, interfacing and bridging the divide between her consciousness and the other realms. The circle represented the multiverse of everything and everyone, and the paths we must take on our journey, sometimes alone, to find our way back to our universal selves.

As Hannah walked the spiral, she began to feel a shift in her consciousness, an awareness beyond herself. In fact, with each step she felt as if she was leaving her self behind, the self that existed in the 3D physical world, to merge with a larger consciousness, a larger vibration, that had no self but was everyone and everything. It was another way of seeing the neural network that the patch had introduced her to. The labyrinth was a healing grid, a web of divine energy. It was bringing her back to wholeness.

Eventually Hannah returned to the manor, the leaves crunching beneath her feet. The tiny muscles in her legs bumped and churned like a bubbling stew. She placed her hand firmly on the doorknob, and when she entered the kitchen, she saw Wendy and her aunt bustling about, still cooking.

"Out for a walk in the afternoon air, love?"

"Yes. I thought I'd take a walk in the forest."

"And what did you find this time?" Jewelia asked hopefully.

"I found a place in the woods I hadn't seen before."

Her aunt set down the wooden spoon in her hand on the counter, giving Hannah her full attention.

"I found this spiral, made of rocks. Is it a labyrinth?"

"Ah yes. I see you are discovering more about Maple Hollow every day," Jewelia replied with a wise look in her eye.

"I know spiritual vortexes are places of awakening, gateways to other dimensions," Hannah said. "Morgan helped me understand that the pumpkins are my portal to the otherworld. But are there other portals? Mirrors, right? Maybe the labyrinth?"

"Of course there are others, my love." Jewelia scooped a large ladle of steaming soup into a small bowl, sliding it toward Hannah. She picked up the spoon again and began stirring the boiling ingredients, spices and herbs mingling together in an orchestra of flavors. As she swirled the spoon in the pot, she began to elaborate: "The spirals are energy centers, similar to the pumpkin patch but different. They are doorways, as well as places where we can refuel our energy. It is a grounding exercise, really. It allows us to tap into the frequency of the island. The stones have been in-fused with energy. The spirals are placed where ley lines intersect. These spots are potent intersections, potent areas of possibility. Our ancestors identified all of these areas on the island when they established Maple Hollow. They infused rocks as protectors and marked the spots with spirals, so that they could return to them whenever they needed to be refueled."

"I see," Hannah said, slurping the hot soup. "I did feel something similar to how I felt when I first arrived on the island, and in the pumpkin patch. A buzzing is the best way I can describe it."

"Each spiral is slightly different, and each has a slightly different purpose. Some heal the heart, while others open the mind. They are in a way programmed to help us heal, so that we can heal others. I'm sure you've heard of the chakras?" Jewelia moved over to the sink to start cleaning the cutting board.

"Yes, I have," Hannah said.

"Well, there are spirals on the island for each chakra, each one special in its power and ability. Those in the outside world cannot see them at all, they are charmed to be visible only to us."

"So, no one else can even see them?" Hannah was surprised at her own ability again.

"Correct. As you know, Hannah, as Healers of the Hollow, we have abilities, powers that have been handed down for thousands of years. They are in our DNA and very, very unique. There are many mysteries in Maple Hollow." Jewelia continued to wash the rest of the utensils at the sink. "Did you ever notice that when water flows, it finds the lowest point and fills it. This isn't always a bad thing. It can be cleansing, releasing, nourishing."

"Was that why, when I saved you, you were in the depths of the sea, deep in the water," Hannah asked.

"Yes. The elements of the earth have connectors for us. Our spirits are here on this earth for a reason. Even though we may not want to be here sometimes, and even though we move through different worlds in our sleep and dreamtime, we are tethered to this physical state. The elements help us navigate the necessity of that connection."

"The dreamworld is definitely another world. Sometimes I feel like I'm traveling to other planes of existence," Hannah offered.

"Below us, and around us, is a silver grid, one we can connect into anytime if we seek it out," Jewelia went on. "There are so many ways to connect. You found the pumpkin patch. It called to you as your first entry point. But there are others, many, many others. The earth can be a magickal place. It offers us a multitude of opportunities to connect. It is your calling now to find the next portal."

She paused and looked Hannah in the eye. "To discover the next entry point to enter the other realms, you don't have to look far, and you can trust you are always in the right place at the right time. But you must open your heart and your mind, so your soul is free to make that connection. You hold the key to unlock these mysteries, Hannah." Jewelia dried the bowls in a circular pattern with the dish towel.

Hannah thought about the dream that had led her to Maple Hollow. The pulsing energetic vines of the pumpkin patch that intertwined around her earthly body, welcomed her in, and filled her spirit with a buzzing energy. It was up to her now to discover what other portals existed on the island in her midst. Those she may not have paid attention to before, but were there all the time around her, waiting to be discovered. Waiting to be tapped. And it seemed that this was now the only way she would find Morgan and save Jezebelle.

CHAPTER TWENTY-EIGHT

THE FIRE

Hannah biked to the Whispering Whiskers Lounge to play piano for the dinner hour. As she rode, the sunset blazed against the sky, splattering bright red and orange streaks like a brilliant painting. She was close to the café when she saw two cats running on the street outside.

Oh no! Some of the cats must have gotten out of the café! was her first thought. She caught up to them on her bike and quickly realized they weren't cats from the café at all. "Merlin! Milu!" she exclaimed. "What are you doing here?" She stopped to caress each of their ears and scratched the side of their face.

Hannah remembered Jewelia telling her once that *familiars never leave their place of protection unless they are in danger.* She began to have a rising feeling that something foreboding had happened.

"Why are you out here?" she asked as she began to follow them down the street. When she got close to Maple Moon, she spotted smoke billowing out of the top windows.

There was no time to think. "Hop in!" she yelled. Merlin and Milu quickly jumped into the basket attached to the front of her bike. Hannah rode straight past the shop and on to the fire station.

"Help! Maple Moon is on fire!" she yelled as she approached the fire house.

There were two firemen standing inside the open garage, winding hoses onto the truck for future use. Their heads popped up when they heard Hannah. They both looked at each other, hopped in the truck, turned the siren on, and whisked off toward the shop.

Hannah followed behind on her bike as fast as she could, Merlin and Milu still bouncing in the basket. The fireman made quick work of putting out the fire, and once it was cleared, Hannah entered the store. Water from the upstairs dousing was leaking down the walls, and it smelled horribly of smoke. Everything was covered in ash and soot.

Hannah went up the stairs toward Morgan's apartment. The walls were etched with dark scratches, flame marks, and chars. It was unlike anything she had ever seen before. Once she made it to the top, she could see that Morgan's home was destroyed. "No wonder Merlin and Milu ran out, those poor souls," she mumbled as she walked around the wreckage, picking up small items here and there to see if anything was salvageable.

The fire chief approached Hannah. "We caught this just in time. The wind must have been blowing it away from us, because we didn't even smell the smoke. Thanks for tipping us off," he said.

"Yes! Well, I had a tip myself, her cats came to tell me."

"Ah, cats. So smart, aren't they?" he said.

Hannah smiled. "The owner, Morgan, she's...out of town at the moment." She hesitated. "I need to go check on the cats. Thanks for your help." Hannah ran back outside to her bike, where Milu and Merlin were waiting.

"I'm so glad you two are okay." Hannah snuggled their furry heads and ears. "You're coming back with me," she said, turning her bike to head back to the manor. She had to let Jewelia know what happened. She stopped at Whispering Whiskers and ran inside to tell Delvina she would have to cancel her shift.

As she made her way back to the manor, many questions swirled in her head. Was the fire set on purpose? If so, who in Maple Hollow would try to destroy Maple Moon? Was this related to the broken mirrors at the manor? There were nefarious forces at work indeed. Hannah rode as fast as she could, the cats digging their claws into the basket and the wind whipping past their whiskers.

"Jewelia! Jewelia!" she yelled as she approached the back door. As soon as she stopped, the cats jumped out of the basket and followed her into the kitchen.

"Yes, love? What did you find?" Jewelia asked, rising from the chair by the fireplace.

"Morgan's apartment! It's destroyed."

Jewelia's eyes widened with disbelief. She stared at the cats. "What? Merlin! Milu!" A look of confusion crossed her face.

"They found me in town and led me to the fire. The whole apartment upstairs is destroyed. I had to ride to the fire station to get help to put it out," Hannah said, talking fast, anxiety in her chest.

"Come here, love, have a seat," Jewelia said, leading her to the armchair she had been sitting in, rubbing her arm in condolence. "This is no accident," Jewelia added, staring into the fire. "Whatever happened to Morgan, I am sure this is related. Merlin, Milu?" She bent over to touch each of the cats. "You will be staying here with us at the manor. It is safest for you here. We've got to get to the bottom of this!" she said, turning to Hannah. The burning intensity of the fire seemed to have transferred to her eyes, which blazed with intention. "Morgan is not safe. She needs our help now more than ever."

Hannah stared into Jewelia's eyes. She could see that her aunt knew deep in her soul that her old friend needed help, from both of them. They were the only ones who could save her.

***

That night, Hannah had a dream she was in the kitchen of the manor, standing in front of the freezer. She had actually stepped inside to hide, from whom she wasn't sure. She tried to close the door behind her so she would be enveloped in darkness. She felt it was the only way the next world would appear. When it did not, she closed the door more tightly. Then she was able to achieve passage and three guides appeared. She wasn't sure who they were, but some of them were people she'd perhaps seen in her childhood or when she was younger.

When Hannah awoke, she began to quickly write down the dream. This time, she decided to give her dream a title. It really centered around the freezer, which had functioned as a portal of sorts to another world where guides awaited her. Was her subconscious trying to put out the fire she'd witnessed at Maple Moon by placing her inside a freezer?

She touched her pen to paper and wrote, *The Frozen Passage*. After recording her dream with as much detail as possible, she began to dig deeper into its meaning. What was the setting? It was the kitchen of the manor. But what association did she have with the kitchen in general? She wasn't much of a cook. Her mind began searching. Then it struck her...of course, she had been in a kitchen when she received the news of her parents' death. That was definitely a unique association with kitchens that most other people would not have.

Next, she considered the objects. The refrigerator, specifically the freezer, was really the focus in the dream. When she'd opened the freezer door, she was trying to hide. Even though she couldn't remember from whom, she definitely could remember the feeling of trying to get away, out of sight, disappearing. She was trying to make herself disappear, but also to make the next world appear. There had been something in her mind that told her if she could completely separate herself from the first world, she could enter the second.

Hannah realized the important object was really the door to the freezer. She had to close it tightly behind her to make the other world appear. In other words, to activate the portal. What could it mean? Maybe she had to leave her past behind in order to move forward?

She pondered what happened next. The alternate otherworld had appeared. It was black on the perimeter, but swirly icy clouds filled the air in the foreground. She had been greeted by three men. She knew in her soul that they meant no harm and were in fact there to guide her. It was almost as if they were each bringing her something. And there had been something a little familiar about one, or maybe two, of them, like she had known them in childhood. Not necessarily as a peer or friend, but perhaps as a mentor.

But who were they? She was not certain of their identity. In fact, she struggled to remember their faces or if any words were spoken. But when she woke up, she felt as if she had been somewhere else. That she had crossed over into an interdimensional place. Could these have been her spirit guides? What were they bringing her, what knowledge? What guidance?

She struggled to remember, but it was fleeting and quickly passing. When she woke up, she had felt a sense of assurance. As if she didn't have to go through this alone. Whatever transition she was passing through, she knew there were others around her to help. Maybe in real life, or maybe in another dimension.

CHAPTER TWENTY-NINE

THE BOX

SEPTEMBER 15, 2009

Hannah spent a long day researching elemental magick and historical lore and trying to put the pieces together. The quicker the minutes passed, the more her worries about Jezebelle and Morgan increased. The stain had now spread up to Jezebelle's shoulders, and her entire arms were filled with the branchy purple veins. Morgan was still missing, and clearly someone or something was trying to destroy all of them.

Hannah thought about the book called *The Land of Brananagh* she had discovered at Morgan's apartment, and the legends she discussed with Ashlin. She remembered the armoire and the turret room and the view of the forest from above. She had a strong feeling that she needed to check the woods again.

She headed toward the forest. She needed to find the Imni tree. A tree unlike any other, a tree that absorbed the world's worries. She needed to see it and relieve herself of her worries. And she had a feeling that the tree lay at the center of it all.

There was so much magick in the forest. As Hannah walked, a dragonfly with wings larger than her hand accompanied her. The trees were like a catacomb, planted at close angles to each other. Each was coated with protective moss, their branches swirling upon each other and creating knotwork patterns as they met. Soft rays of the late afternoon sun slanted into the woods from above, dappling the clearings with a warm yellow glow.

Fireflies were all around. Tiny orbs of all different colors glowed in the darkness under the trees, floating about on the air, light and without a care. A soft stream flowed near the path where Hannah walked. The water ever so gently grazed the smooth river rocks beneath.

She focused her memory on *The Land of Brananagh*. She could still see the words on the page:

Worries big and small fuel the tree, transforming into growth and food. The transference between humans and nature benefits both sides. Worriers aren't poisoning the tree; rather, it exists to transfer energy, sending it down to the earth through its roots. As a healing tree, its roots serve as transmutation channels, running the negativity back into the earth to be broken down and reinvented, taking the energy back into the cycle of the land.

Hannah stopped in front of a tall tree with sprawling roots. Etched into the bark were thick lines, like the ones she had seen in her dream about Leaf. The firefly seemed to have led her there to join the rest of its family, which circled thickly around it. She sat down at the base of the tree, feeling burdened by the heavy weight of worry, and decided to experiment. She envisioned herself walking among lush green trees on a dewy path, carrying her worries. The grand tree above her, with its radiating branches and roots, was ready for the transfer.

She began to pour out her worries to the tree, and as she did, she imagined that the branches began to glisten, each tiny leaf on the tree sparkling. Eventually the entire tree began to glow. The more she dumped out her worries, the more beautiful and bright was the tree.

After a few minutes, Hannah opened up her eyes and looked up at the tree. To her amazement, it was fully illuminated like bright stars in a galaxy, shimmering and joyous. Was it the fireflies, or was this the fabled Imni tree?

As she headed back, the tree slowly dimmed behind her, Hannah felt lighter and relieved. She thought about Jewelia's statement that every woman's magick on the island was unique, and now, more than ever, she felt as if she was getting a glimpse into Morgan's enchanting world of the woods.

At the manor she grabbed her bike and rode into town, headed toward the library.

"Well, hello!" Ashlin said. She was outside taking boxes of books off a delivery truck.

"Ashlin, do you have time to chat?" Hannah asked softly.

"Of course," Ashlin said, her interest piqued. She walked over to open the door for Hannah, flipping the sign from *Open* to *Closed*.

They sat side-by-side on a bench. "I'm curious…what powers do other Healers on Maple Hollow have?" Hannah asked. "I only know about my family, Morgan, Wendy, and you. Maybe there are other powers that could help us."

"That's a great question, and one all seekers eventually come to. We are all connected through a neural network, so our powers are all connected, but our proximity and DNA gives us talents for certain specialties, which might differ." Ashlin walked across the room, heading toward one of the bookshelves in the science section. "Do you know much about quantum physics?" she asked, pulling a book from the shelf.

"Hmm. I've heard of it, but no, not really."

"Here's some reading you can take with you." Ashlin passed her a book with *Quantum Entanglement* on the cover.

"Ooh, this looks interesting," Hannah said, intrigued.

"Like the roots and vines, theories of quantum physics help explain both how we are connected and, conversely, how some become disconnected. Physicists call this 'coherence' and 'decoherence.' You'll find that we all have abilities innate in us, but sometimes we can't access them. That's really what may be our purpose in this incarnation, to discover and make that connection."

On the way back from the library, Hannah thought about her parents again. What if their experience was dimensionally intertwined with hers?

Once she arrived back at the manor, she ran up to her bedroom, opened her closet, and reached into the back for the dusty box she had placed there two years prior when she'd moved in with her aunt. It had been given to her by her grandmother when her parents passed away. But she'd always felt like there was something she wasn't being told about that whole situation. It had led her to have a great sense of distrust of anyone in uniform, especially detectives or the police. It made her resolute in the necessity of discovering the truth on her own. It made her always skeptical, and drawn to uncover what was hidden.

Hannah opened the box and started sifting through the contents. The first thing she pulled out was her father's calendar, then a framed picture of herself and her grandmother. There was a small medal she had won in grade school for the school talent show, then her mother's dressy elbow-length gloves, and brochures from trips they had taken. Beneath these was a small stack of newspaper clippings. They were all about the accident.

She read the headline, *Tragic Accident off Lone Peak Cliff*, dated October 18, 1987, and then just stared at the faded and now fragile piece of paper, browned from years of air exposure. She could remember it like it was yesterday, even though it was over twenty years ago. Their car had mysteriously driven off Lone Peak Cliff, crashing into the rocks below.

"No one could survive that drop," one of the detectives had said.

She looked at the different clippings. Some had pictures of the car, some of the top of the cliff. Now that she knew more about her family legacy, Hannah's understanding of what had happened that night had begun to reassemble. She'd come into the knowledge that there were nefarious forces in the universe, including the Dream Haunters, who target unsuspecting victims, specifically her family. It was as if she was looking down at the situation from a much higher perspective now and could see a larger picture that previously had been obscured, a 360-degree view. What if the Dream Haunters had tried to kill her parents? They had tried to kill her and Jewelia, so why not them?

Then her thoughts leapt to the next logical step, an idea that she had never given herself permission to pursue. What if her parents weren't dead at all? What if they had just been trapped by the Dream Haunters and dematerialized, like her aunt that fateful night of the giant storm? If she'd saved Jewelia from the dark desolation of her nightmare, could she save her parents as well?

Thinking back to how she'd uncovered the mystery of her aunt's disappearance, a veritable light bulb glowed in Hannah's mind. Of course! She pushed aside the box in her bedroom and ran down the stairs to the library. She was looking for *Mercury Retrograde Compendium*. She remembered that it had a calendar in the back of all instances of Mercury retrograde for the last fifty years. Retrograde had weakened her aunt's powers, which was why the Dream Haunters had used that period to their advantage to trap her. What if it had been Mercury retrograde when her parents died?

Hannah pushed open the door under the stairway and made her way down the short hall into the library. As she entered, she searched her mind for the books she had paid such close attention to two years ago. She pulled the rolling ladder close to her, climbed on with both feet, and began searching the volumes.

Then her eyes caught the title on the spine. This was it!

She flipped to the back for the almanac of dates and scanned down for the year 1987. *Mercury Retrograde: February 18–March 12; June 21–July 15 ...*

When she got to the end of the list, Hannah's jaw dropped in shock. Why had she not looked this up before? There it was, inked onto the page. The confirmation she'd always been looking for. The final dates of Mercury retrograde in 1987 were October 16–November 6.

The morning her grandmother had woken her up with the news of her parents' death was the morning of October 17. The car accident happened the night of October 16. That would have been the second night of Mercury retrograde.

Jewelia's words from two years prior now echoed in her mind: *"The rare synchronicity of Halloween and Mercury retrograde, the thinning veil combined with the planetary influence, created a portal that allowed the Dream Haunters to traverse the boundary that usually exists between the worlds and shapeshift into ours. They were able to use this to their advantage."*

Her eyes wide, Hannah continued to stare at the page in shock and disbelief. So not only had her parents' accident happened during Mercury retrograde, but in 1987, as in 2007, retrograde had coincided with Halloween, the rare synchronicity. This meant that the Dream Haunters could have shapeshifted into existence.

It was all so obvious, now that she had put the pieces together. It was clear these same nefarious forces had been at work when her parents died. Her intuition was right. The Dream Haunters had something to do with the accident. They could have killed her parents. Or…just like with her aunt, her parents might in fact not be dead at all.

***

That night, having read through all the newspaper clippings, Hannah had a dream about her father. She found herself standing at the edge of a large cliff. Her feet started to fumble on the crumbled rocks at the stony edge as she peered over. She kept looking over the edge of the cliff and could see small rocks tumbling. She felt fear creeping into her body. They were standing together at the precipice, looking out to the sea.

"Are you okay?" her father asked.

"Yes," she replied.

She tried to remind herself that she was light, like an angel, not heavy with worry. Then she looked up. The sky was filled with towering curtains of multi-colored rays. The green and purple lights danced as their reflection perfectly mirrored in the water below. Time moved slowly as they stood on the edge, watching the shimmering lights.

Suddenly the scene shifted and she saw a vision of a little girl riding her bike down the main hallway in the manor. She followed, heading toward the parlor. The distant call of the piano sending its notes floating toward her. When she entered, her eyes went directly to the bench: on it sat Wixby.

"Hannah!" he exclaimed.

"Wixby, where have you been?!" she said, both happy and surprised.

"I had to help out some of my other friends, but I made sure guides were there to help you."

"You sent Leaf and Filgrim?" Hannah asked.

"Of course. We're all part of the Hollow," he replied.

"I just had this dream I was on a cliff," Hannah said, lifting him up and setting him on her lap. "It was night, but the sky was so bright. It was moving, swirling almost, in a comforting wave."

"Like a rainbow?" he asked.

"Sort of," Hannah replied, "but more like glistening curtains in the sky, waves amongst the stars. My father was there, and he asked me if I was okay."

"Your father?" Wixby echoed.

"Yes, he passed away when I was younger. Well, both my parents did. It was an accident, on Lone Peak Cliff." She paused.

"I see," the cat said, his eyes getting wide.

"Years after it happened, I used to go to the edge of the cliff. Scanning the horizon for some shred of evidence. But everything was likely long washed away by the tide. I've never gotten closure. I still have so many questions about what happened."

"What would you name the dream?" Wixby asked.

"I guess I would call it *The Cliff of Hope*," Hannah said slowly.

"What was most important about it?" he prompted.

"To me, the emotional journey was most important. At first, I felt unsafe at the edge, my feet shuffling in the small rocks that tumbled to the sea below. I felt like I had to watch myself, make sure I didn't get too bogged down. That I didn't fall off the cliff myself. I carry a heaviness sometimes in my soul, in the dark parts of my mind. But after I spoke with my father and looked up at the sky, that went away."

"Then you felt peaceful?"

"Yes. I was filled with the sense that my father was watching over me, reaching out to me. That both of my parents were with me, that their spirits were dancing around me. The more I thought about being lifted up, the lighter I felt."

"Like you're together all the time," Wixby said knowingly.

"Yes. I guess I can visit them in my dreamworld, at least, since dreams are beyond space and time."

"Then what happened?"

"Then the scene totally shifted and I saw an image of a girl on a bike. She was riding down the hallway in the manor. In fact, she led me here!"

"Who was the girl?"

"I can't say for sure, but it reminded me of a dream I had years ago about a child who lost her mittens and they became a kite. To me, it serves as a reminder to always keep the connection I had as an innocent, albeit naïve, child.

"Connection to what?"

"To light," Hannah said, with a sparkle in her eyes.

"What does it mean?" Wixby mused.

Hannah sat in contemplation for a moment. "The cliff is a metaphor with strong ties to my parents. The sky...well, now that I think of it, it was the aurora borealis! And the Northern Lights are the homeland of Arianrhod, the Celtic goddess who shapeshifts into an owl. It all makes sense! The owl, the leaf, and the dragonflies led me to the Imni tree, to finally be free of my worries. I had asked my spirit guides to show me, and they did through their elemental magick of air. They all were meant to show me how to be light, how to fly, how to become one with the elements. It was a mystical converging of the earth, in the form of the cliff, and the air, in the form of the guides of the sky, all of it reflected in the mirror of the sea's brilliant reflection."

Hannah sat still, a profound feeling of understanding sweeping over her.

"Well done," Wixby said, tapping his tail.

CHAPTER THIRTY

THE WELL

SEPTEMBER 16, 2009

Hannah slowly roused herself from sleep and transcribed the dreams in her journal. She had talked with Wixby in a dream within a dream.

But as she became more awake, her remembered she had little time to save Jezebelle. At the pace the stain was moving, it could reach her heart within twenty-four hours. Hannah remembered the message of her dream, that she must embody the light. She returned to the library downstairs. An eerie glow of purple filled the large windows, the morning fog obscuring whatever lurked outside. She took the matches from the mantle and, grabbing a candelabra, struck the match against the cast-iron base and proceeded to light each candle one by one.

There was no light in the room besides the flickering golden glow from the candles. The light of the flames illuminated the table upon which the candelabra sat, creating a ring of light by which to view the *Grimoire de Skye*. She had brought it up from the secret room yesterday to delve into its magick, its secrets. She suspected that since she was able to banish the Dream

Haunters with the magick of the pumpkin patch, she must also hold the key to banish the Illusionix through the Dream Mirrors. The *Grimoire de Skye* lay open upon the table; she hoped she could once again rely on its penchant for having a mind of its own and opening to what one sought or needed.

She heard distant notes cascading into the library from the direction of the great hall. Aunt Jewelia was playing the grand organ. It filled the manor with a sea of sound, raising their vibration, opening the doorway of answers and hopefully awakening Jezebelle from her stupor and paralysis.

On her way down the stairs, Hannah had chosen a mirror from the wall, and she now placed it before her on the table beyond the grimoire. The purple glow from the windows and golden glow from the flames mixed in the reflection. Because the mirrors were being used as a portal for darkness to enter, she would have to find a way to meet whatever lay on the other side, beyond her reflection. It was the only way to prevent the Illusionix from controlling the portal.

As the grimoire flipped open to the page she was seeking, she saw the words *Tástáil Tairseach*. She pulled out her phone and slowly typed the words into the translation bar. "Portal testing," she read aloud. On the page were diagrams that appeared to indicate a way to test for a portal. The book indicated that if a key or ring was held above an object, such as a mirror, and began to spin in circles, that indicated a portal. It also showed a diagram of two mirrors facing each other and explained that two mirrors could form a vortex within themselves.

Midnight jumped up and sat next to the grimoire, his eyes glowing in the candlelight and tail flipping off the edge of the table. Hannah reached around her neck, unhooking the chain of her long, silver necklace on which hung the key her aunt had gifted her. She held the chain in her hand, the key dangling over the mirror. In silence, she watched and waited.

The key began to spiral on its own, circling as if by some unseen force, confirming the presence of a portal. Observing the other diagram, Hannah began to wonder if perhaps a mirror vortex might be the way to trap the nefarious spirit of the Illusionix.

Hannah ran out of the library, down the long, dark hallway and out the back door of the kitchen toward the pumpkin patch. She knew that to save both Morgan and Jezebelle, she had to tweak her methods, approach her rescue a new and different way. The grimoire had showed her how to test for portals. She already knew the pumpkin patch was a portal, of course. But to pass into the realm where she could vanquish the Illusionix, she had to manifest yet another portal, one that didn't naturally exist but would come into existence by intentional circumstance.

She stood for a moment, closed her eyes, and scanned the patch, paying close attention to small sensations passing from the vines into her body through her feet. Merlin and Milu had followed her outside. They seemed to each be searching for clues, sniffing out what was unseen.

Opening her eyes, Hannah quickly selected a pumpkin and detached it from the vine. A spark tingled in her hands as she grasped the stem. Then she immediately sat down among the vines, placing her hands on the pumpkin and calming her breath. As wound up as she was, she knew she had to control her mind, focus, and go deep, as Morgan had shown her.

As she sat cross-legged, her eyes closed, with her hands on the pumpkin, Hannah felt the subtle sensation of something in her lap. A slight smile crossed her lips as she realized it was Merlin, come to accompany her on her journey to the dreamworld. As she waited for a vision to appear in her mind, she slowly began to see a network below the ground.

It was like a maze, but filled with insects, snails, and worms, all snaking and foraging about. They were working to encase, encompass, entrap something. As she watched the network of earthly insects circling, she waited, observing. *What is happening here? What are you showing me?* she said in her mind, asking the earth dwellers of the underground.

As her vision scanned from the depths of the soil to the tops of the earth, she saw large stone monoliths rising out of the ground. It was then that Hannah realized what she was seeing—they were gravestones.

"The cemetery!" Hannah exclaimed, breaking her concentration. "Morgan is trapped in the cemetery!"

She jumped up from where she was sitting and ran with both cats out of the patch. The Skye family cemetery was deep in the woods. It may not have been in a forest when it was first established, but long ago they planted a tree next to each gravestone, so over time a forest had grown around the stones. The cemetery was now in its own deep wood that encompassed and encased the stones.

When Hannah reached the cemetery, she sought shelter under a large maple tree. Although the graveyard was not large, there were probably fifty or more headstones. Some were just plaques on the ground marking the spot. But others were large. Some had fallen over and were crumbling on the ground, worn and weathered from the wind and rain, gradually returning to the earth like the soil that held them.

"Múscail Fíniúnacha," Hannah chanted, the words dropping from her lips to the earth below.

As she concentrated, she summoned the assistance of the tree roots. They began to snake and twist around her ankles. Just like in her recurring dream of the pumpkin patch, she felt a tingling sensation begin to rise in her body. It was like her feet had stepped into a cold pool, or an icy breeze had sent a shimmer down her spine. Except this time something different was happening. She could hear sounds of crackling and rustling coming from the edge of the forest. It was the maple roots awakening. Morgan's connection to the trees of the island, and her ancestral magick, were summoning the assistance of the woods.

Roots began to extend from each tree, burrowing across the ground at rapid speed, breaking up the soil all around her until a large hole in the ground appeared. It was an old well that was buried within the cemetery. Merlin and Milu ran to the hole and began digging with their paws. As Hannah watched, she began to see something in the soil, first fingers, then a hand. The fingers were attempting to free themselves from the dirt. Hannah stifled a scream.

"Morgan?!" she exclaimed, running toward the hole. As she desperately began to clear away the soil, first a hand, then an arm, appeared.

"Morgan, is that you?" She cleared the dirt away frantically. Eventually a shoulder emerged, then silver hair.

"Morgan!" Hannah cried as she finally cleared the soil away and pulled her from the hole out onto the grass. "Morgan, can you hear me?"

Morgan's eyes began to blink, slowly at first. Then her eyes fixed upon Hannah. "Hannah?" she said with a croak, as if she had been asleep a thousand years.

"Morgan, are you okay?"

"I was dreaming. How did I get here?" Morgan asked weakly.

Hannah reached out her hand to Morgan as the cats continued to clear away the soil, and as she did so, she had a lightbulb realization. Underneath her nails was dirt. In her furious digging to rescue Morgan, the soil had gotten packed under her nails. Images flashed in her mind of Jezebelle's nails and the mysterious substance underneath them.

"Soil!" she said out loud.

"What?" Morgan asked.

"That's what's under Jezebelle's nails!"

"Jezebelle? Oh, my dear, I was supposed to be watching her. Is she okay?"

"She will be now," Hannah said in a determined tone as she helped Morgan to her feet. The realization that the substance under Jezebelle's nails was soil prompted another thought. Could Jezebelle have been digging by the Imni Tree? She helped Morgan dust off her clothes.

"Merlin, Milu, my babies! What are you doing here?" Morgan exclaimed, grabbing both of the cats and holding them close.

"They came to find me…Morgan, there's something I need to tell you," Hannah said with much trepidation. How could she tell Morgan that her entire home had been destroyed when she'd only just brought her back? "Maple Moon…there was a fire," Hannah began.

"What?!" Morgan was suddenly much more awake, and held the cats closer to her chest.

"Merlin and Milu, they led me to it. I'd been going to feed them since you've been gone. Yes, you've been gone a week. But they had always stayed at the apartment. One day, I saw smoke coming out of the windows of the shop and found them on the street."

Morgan's gaze faded, a lost look crossing her face. "But who would do such a thing?" she finally asked.

"Morgan," Hannah started, as she began walking her back to the manor, "could you have been trapped by the Dream Haunters? Have you been recording your dreams?"

"Oh dear, I haven't been in a few weeks. But there's no overlap between Halloween and Mercury retrograde this year, so the celestial alignment isn't powerful enough for them to manifest into human form. They certainly couldn't have set my shop on fire."

"C'mon, let's go back to the manor," Hannah said. She placed her arm around Morgan and walked with her back across the grounds.

When they arrived, Jewelia ran out of the kitchen. "Morgan! You've come back!" she said, hugging her in relief and leading her to a kitchen chair. Suddenly Hannah remembered her parents' death, announced in the kitchen. And now here she sat, on a hard wooden chair once again, delivering foreboding news.

"We've been researching and trying everything since you've been gone to help Jezebelle, and we think we know who is after her."

"Who?" Morgan asked.

"It's an ancient evil force called the Illusionix. Jewelia and I learned about it from the grimoire. It's poisoning Jezebelle, and it tried to attack us through the mirrors."

"The Illusionix," Morgan said profoundly, a searching look coming into her eyes. "But how do we fight it? How do we protect ourselves and cure Jezebelle?"

Hannah realized that the one woman who had all the answers was now asking her for them. It really was up to her to solve this mystery and help protect the other Healers of the Hollow.

"I went to the pumpkin patch, to try to use the pumpkins to see where you were," she explained. "My vision led me to the cemetery. Once there, I did a spell to activate the vines. But it activated the roots of the trees."

"I was having a nightmare I was buried alive, underground," Morgan remembered. "And then you saved me." She smiled at Hannah. Then she looked stricken. "Trapped by the trees!" she said in a ghostly realization.

"Yes," Hannah continued, "but it wasn't a nightmare! It was an illusion, a false reality. The roots of the Imni tree transformed your emotions, releasing you. Then Merlin and Milu helped me dig you out."

"Oh, my dears, I love them so much," she said, hugging their furry bodies again.

"Come now," Jewelia said, standing up. "They will try to trap and destroy all of us. We must stop it!"

"But how?" Morgan asked again.

"We must summon the Illusionix directly and destroy it," Hannah said, her tone resolute as she rose and walked toward the library.

"Hannah, love..." Jewelia trailed off. "Morgan, why don't you make yourself comfortable in the parlor? You've certainly been through enough." She led Morgan to retire on the large Victorian sofa. Morgan collapsed onto the purple velvet, weakened from her battle and trauma. Merlin and Milu jumped to snuggle up next to her. Jewelia quickly left the parlor and followed Hannah to the library.

When Jewelia entered, Hannah was pacing back and forth. "The black mirrors we had at the dinner party…where did you put them?" she asked Jewelia.

"In a dark place, one where they can only be found when needed," Jewelia replied. She stepped on a creaky floorboard and pulled a book toward her on the bookshelf. The bookshelf began to slowly open toward them, revealing a dark passageway.

"Another secret passageway?" Hannah said in surprise. She thought the trap door in the library was the only one.

"Yes, my love. They are everywhere in the manor," Jewelia said as she walked into the darkness, Hannah following close behind.

They traveled down a long hallway. The only light came from small lanterns perched on the walls on either side. In between them were the mirrors, the ones they had used at the 999 dinner party that night. Seeing them all in a row gave Hannah a rather ominous feeling. It was as if they were a series of doorways or soldiers, waiting for their orders. Their glass was dark and black, as if no reflection could be seen.

"We keep them here to protect them," Jewelia said. "They are not for the eyes of the faint of heart. Only those ready to see will see. Pick one that calls to you, and I will do the same."

A few moments later, they were walking toward the light of the library. Hannah emerged holding her mirror, wondering if she had chosen it or if it had chosen her.

"What are you hoping to do with the mirrors?" Jewelia asked.

"I have a plan," Hannah said. "We'll have to see if it works. We know the Illusionix may come back now that Morgan is free. We know Jezebelle was trapped by the Illusionix. I figure it should be easy to summon it right now. Then I will capture it and send it back to where it came from," she declared. She tilted her head and listened intently. "Come with me, Aunt Jewelia! A storm is coming." Hannah ran out of the library, Jewelia right behind her.

They each grabbed a cloak from a hook by the back door and headed out into the wind, Jewelia leading them through the forest. Dark clouds began to creep in from the distant skies beyond the manor. The sweet, dewy smell of approaching rain filled the air as the leaves on the maple trees waved and flipped, turning their veins toward the sky. The forecast had been calling for storms all week, and Hannah knew she needed to be ready. Storms could wield so much power, such incredible calamities of force, as she'd experienced firsthand with the Skye Mirror. Storms created change whether one was ready for it or not. Her parents, her aunt, and Morgan had all been affected by a storm. Low, heavy rumbles of thunder began to echo in the distance. She knew the storm would bring her answers.

"First, we will both gaze into a black mirror, like we did the night of the dinner party. Since we know the Illusionix is near, this will hopefully summon it. Then, once it arrives and the storm peaks, we will turn our mirrors toward each other and capture the Illusionix within the mirror vortex, destroying it with its own reflection."

"Brilliant," Jewelia said.

"But we have to wait for the storm to get closer," Hannah said as a lightning bolt streaked across the sky above them.

"Let's count the distance," Jewelia whispered. They each began to count quietly under their breath, the figments of spoken numbers falling from their lips.

"One, two, three, four ..." Then came a distant roll of thunder that quickened their hearts, halting their count.

"It's close," Hannah said, nodding and looking at Jewelia. They each held up the mirror to their face.

Hannah knew that to capture the Illusionix, she had to deflect it soon after summoning it. She gazed into the black mirror, bracing herself for what she might see.

She tried to clear her mind. She didn't want to impose anything on the mirror. She just wanted to allow it to present whatever she needed to see at that exact moment in time. As her mind quieted and she focused on her breathing, a scene began to form in her mind.

Hannah saw herself old and alone, poor and struggling. The manor was worn, the grounds no longer kept up. She was all by herself in the world, preyed upon by demons. Her will was broken, her powers depleted. A tear emerged from her eye and she began to wonder if this was her fate. She almost began to believe it was truly a glimpse into a predetermined future. She was going to be old, alone, and weak. She knew she had reached her dark place.

At that moment, another roll of thunder arrived and she felt something around her ankles. It was Midnight, walking over her feet and trying to remind her what she was witnessing. Illuminating the frailty of the spectacle, the projection of her worst fears, the falsity of the illusion.

Remembering why she had looked in the mirror in the first place, Hannah sprang into action. "Face the mirrors!" she yelled, attempting to jar Jewelia from whatever darkness she had been drawn into.

But Jewelia didn't move. She too had fallen prey to the illusions in the mirror; her eyes held a look of sorrow and defeat as they fixed upon it.

"Jewelia, now!" Hannah yelled, but it was as if Jewelia could not hear her.

"See beyond! It's an illusion!" she yelled. Then Midnight sunk his claws into Jewelia's feet, jarring her from her trance. The fog began to swirl around them both, and as they watched, it began to enter the mirrors, first slowly, then like a funnel stream.

Not flinching, Hannah began to chant: "*Ag glaoch ar mo shinsi., Bris an Illusion seo. Féach ar M'Anam.*"

A large lightning bolt struck the ground directly between them.

As she recited the words from the ancient grimoire, she realized she was asking the universe to show her not what the Illusionix wanted her to see, but what her soul knew to be true. She was harnessing the flash of light to dispel the illusion, defeat the false reality, and dismantle the hallucination, conquering it forever.

The heavy fog began to gather around her. It obscured Midnight near her ankles and rose up toward her head, wrapping in a spiral around her mouth. But as it met the words from her lips, the trajectory of the fog was rerouted. Instead of penetrating her skin and mind, it was headed into the mirror behind her. It was flowing away from her. The illusion's transit had been disrupted, redirected away from her consciousness and safely into the beyond.

"Fill ar an Dorchadas!" Hannah yelled. It was the same incantation she had used to destroy the Dream Haunters, sending them back to the darkness. A funnel of smoke and fog like a tower appeared between herself and Jewelia. As they held their mirrors, the fog was sucked into each mirror. Then there was a large blast and they both fell back, blinded by the light. The mirrors fell to the ground, shattering the black glass into tiny broken pieces.

"Hannah, you did it once again!" Jewelia exclaimed. She stepped carefully across the broken glass to hug her niece.

"It worked!" Hannah replied with relief.

"You destroyed the Illusionix. It went back through the mirror. You discovered that the demon of the Illusionix is nothing but the reflection of one's own blocks, fears, and attachments. By demanding that the illusion be broken, and that your true soul be seen, you dissolved all of its power back into the shadow. Quick, let's go check on Jezebelle!"

They both ran into the manor and up the stairs to the room where Jezebelle had lain immobile for so long. When they pushed open the door, there was Jezebelle, sitting up in her bed, holding a cup in one hand and rubbing her eyes with the other, as she woke from her long stupor. Wendy was sitting by her side, a smile across her face.

"Jezebelle!" Hannah exclaimed.

"Hannah? Jewelia?" Jezebelle replied with joy and confusion. "What happened?"

"Easy now, love," Jewelia said, approaching her and placing her hand on her shoulder. "You've been through a lot." She sat down next to her on the bed while Hannah stood in the doorway. "That night, at the dinner party, do you remember what happened?" she asked gently.

"I'm sorry, Jewelia. This is all my fault."

Jewelia and Hannah looked at each other in surprise.

"I researched the island of Maple Hollow before I came here," Jezebelle said softly. "I learned that your island has its own ecosystem, unlike anywhere else. I also learned of the legend of a flower that extends youth. I selfishly wanted it for myself. When I discovered that the manor had its own greenhouse of rare plants, I knew that visiting you with Wendy would be the perfect cover for me to access it undetected. So naturally I was thrilled to receive your dinner party invitation to visit Skye Manor."

Jezebelle looked apologetically at them all. "The night of your party, I was supposed to help Wendy with the catering, but instead, I slipped out of the kitchen and into the greenhouse. With Mr. Adams busy serving drinks in the parlor, there was no one on the grounds. I found the white-petaled flower that only blooms in the darkness, fabled to provide eternal beauty. Concerned I would be caught, and to leave no trace, I quickly ate some, taking more for later. I figured this was a harmless indulgence, a little appetizer to the larger meal with a much bigger benefit. But once the third course was completed, I realized something was wrong. My face became hot and red, my stomach twisted into painful knots, and my head swooned so badly I could barely hold my mirror."

With a blush, Jezebelle confessed, "I started to panic. When the lights went out, I knew it was my only chance to escape the party without being discovered. I ran into the woods and found a large tree to bury the flowers under, but my muscles were beginning to seize. I ran with every effort I could muster, but then everything went black."

"What you consumed was not the fabled petals of beauty, but rather a poisonous nightshade," Jewelia explained. "A simple mistake, but the toxin causes horrific cramping."

"Of course! It all makes sense now," Hannah interjected. "The doorway to Phantasm was opened the night of the eclipse. In fact, Leaf and the owls have been warning me all along in my dreams! With the portal open, the Illusionix was able to materialize into physical form as the fog, which destroyed the mirrors and came after us at the manor. Jezebelle's distress unknowingly conjured the Imni tree, and it manifested to consume her worries. But she was ignorant to its power and instead attempted to bury the evidence of her vanity, disturbing the base of the tree, the portal to Phantasm."

"Yes," Jewelia chimed in. "Many have sought the legendary yet illusive flower known only as *áilleacht*, which some say promises eternal beauty. But the manor is betwixt by many poisonous flora, planted by our ancestors as a protective shield. The one you consumed is part of the Narcissus genus." Jewelia placed a consoling hand over Jezebelle's. "I appreciate your honesty. Do not feel ashamed, as we all have our demons. We all strive and struggle. What's important is that you finally were released from your illusion. Now you have seen the truth and realized that you no longer need nor want eternal beauty. Our physical bodies are just a shell for our spirits. All true beauty lies within."

Morgan appeared at the doorway, having overheard Jezebelle's confession. "The Imni tree serves as the container for all the world's worries. But the roots are toxic to anyone that disturbs them. They will be poisoned by Imobium, the lethal substance which courses in the roots, thick with the worries of the world. You see, my dear, in order to embrace your soul's true path, you had to first experience a metaphysical death. It was not a death in the physical sense, but rather in the mystical sense. The death of the ego, which is an illusory creation of our human experience. The ego keeps us from following our true path. It averts our eyes from our own path to watch another's. It whispers in our ear that we are not good enough, that we need the knowledge of another, rather than allowing us to listen to our own inner wisdom. It demotes our sense of self until we feel empty and listless, directionless, uninspired."

"Ah, of course, your sinister sickness was caused by Imobium. First your muscles seizing, then your organs, then finally your mind. It all shut down and you were paralyzed like a stone, frozen into the pose you landed in. Etched in that moment of panic forever," Jewelia concluded.

"Morgan, you're back!" Wendy gasped, finally finding her voice.

Morgan smiled at her and continued. "It is easier to replicate what someone else is doing, judge our success by their accomplishments, and gauge our worth based on the quantified value someone else has established. There is comfort in the assessment, the baseline that we intrinsically feel we can't attain. It keeps us safe and small. But it is our duty as we walk this human experience to see the ego for what it is, to learn to sap its power, to reverse the polarity of our existence and switch the balance in our soul's favor. To refuse to listen any longer to the self-sabotaging falsities the ego attempts to have us believe."

Wendy was nodding, fully understanding Morgan and Jewelia's wisdom. Jezebelle, Jewelia, Morgan, and Hannah all retreated downstairs to the kitchen. Wendy had cooked up a huge pot of veggie stew and bustled about preparing to serve it up.

"That looks delicious, dear," Morgan said to her, a twinkle in her eye.

"Are you okay?" Wendy asked.

"Always," Morgan said as she leaned over to pick up a pot of tea Wendy had just brewed. She carried it over to the table with stacked mini cups. She patted the chair adjacent to her to invite Hannah to take her place.

Everyone ate their fill of crusty cornbread loaves and steamy stew until their sides nearly burst. Then, one by one, they sauntered upstairs to their rooms.

***

Hannah tossed and turned that night until her body finally gave way and she found herself in a dream.

She was running in the woods. The thunder crashed around her as her feet fell heavily upon the wet, hard soil. She wasn't even sure if she was running to something or away from something. But she was filled with a sense of fear that made her lungs feel tight, her chest feel constricted. With each step she took, her lungs ached for more air, but there wasn't time to expand them to let more in.

Up ahead, she saw a dark shadow emerging from the trees. It was the icehouse, buried in the depths of the forest. Her feet slowed as she approached, the small ominous building blocking her path. Then the woods suddenly began to clear around her, almost in a circular fashion, as if they were being wiped off the canvas in a cyclone. She looked up and saw above her the wide-open night sky. She stood for a moment, admiring the twinkling stars and the glory of the moonglow.

Then it emerged. The most beautiful colors, all gathered into a prominent band in the sky. It was a rainbow in the dark of night. Glowing like none she had ever seen.

CHAPTER THIRTY-ONE

THE LIGHTNING

SEPTEMBER 17, 2009

The next morning, Hannah and Jewelia stood in front of the large bay window of the library, side by side, looking out to the sea. Waves tousled about, crashing into one another.

"Storms are so unpredictable," Jewelia remarked. "Even though as humans we try to claim we can predict the weather, in fact, we cannot. Have you ever looked at the weather report and it said sunny, only to have a sudden cloudburst rain down from the sky?"

"Of course, and it will inevitably be while I'm on my bike," Hannah said smirking.

"Exactly," her aunt said. "It would seem like such an inopportune time, an unfortunate coincidence, bad timing, some would say. But the truth of it is, the weather is intrinsically tied with our energy. Have you ever had an emotional release only to have hail suddenly emerge from the clouds? That is your energy materializing in the very vapor that surrounds us. When you are seemingly caught in the rain, it is actually a cleansing for you. In other words, you are meant to be in that rain, your skin made wet by the moisture from the sky. Your head is cleansed, your spirit, too."

Jewelia peered out the window at the sky. "Energetically, lightning is not bad, but it holds so much energy it can be used for bad or good. Lightning itself is a portal. As you've discovered, there are so many portals around us all the time; it is just a matter of being able to see them. When the veil is thinner between the worlds, it is easier for us to recognize and access the portals. But it also makes it easier for other spirits as well, not all of them with good intent. This is the balance. The balance between good and evil, light and dark," said Jewelia.

"I always wondered if the weather had another purpose, another meaning, beyond just being a daily occurrence," Hannah replied.

"Of course. Why do you think we have so many metaphors that blend the weather with our emotions?"

"And so, when there is lightning, what does that mean about our emotions?"

"The most strong and powerful emotions bring lightning," Jewelia said. "They hold so much potential waiting to be unleashed. That night long ago when I was trapped by the Dream Haunters, there was so much lightning in the sky, and the winds were swirling so forcefully around me. At the time, it had seemed like I was fighting the storm, but I was actually fighting the storm within myself. The inner struggle I'd always had between my inner voices. The one that told me I must do everything myself, and the one that told me to ask for help. The one that believed only I must bear the burdens of the family legacy, and the other that whispered that help was right in front of my eyes if I could only see it. That was why I finally wrote the letter to you, breaking the silence once and for all."

***

That night in a dream, Hannah was running out into the night, the sky brewing with an approaching storm. As she looked up between the forest branches, she saw in the sky a multitude of flashing bolts of lightning. Then the sky seemed to open up and a collection of lightning bands bonded together into a stream that spilled over like a waterfall, and then cascaded down toward the ground. When it reached the soil, the lightning spread out like a large hand, each finger extending streams of glowing blue and white blinding energy. She knew it was coming toward her, that she would soon be enveloped by it, that it would inhabit and infuse her. And soon after that, it did.

It was as if she were standing near a live wire, where the electricity needed to activate the surrounding area. She did not even need to touch it directly. She felt it first in her feet, then almost immediately the glow was emanating from her eyes.

Her whole body was pulsating and filled with a blue-white powerful glow, her body lifted off the ground until she was floating on her back. Hannah felt a breeze coming up from the ground beneath her, pushing her toward the sky, filling her with effortless peace. She wanted to dwell there, in that floating, wonderful empowered feeling of calm and renewal. She had discovered that the storms were not just part of nature, but also part of her. She was one with the elements.

EPILOGUE

Hannah woke up with a feeling of excitement in her chest. She reached for *Dream Awakening* and rapidly flipped through its pages, this time reading the words. A flush of validation came over her when she saw, written in ink, the exact steps she had walked herself when interpreting her dream with Wixby. She *had* successfully read the book with her mind. She *had* absorbed all of its wisdom, but without reading it. She *had* invented her own way of understanding her dreams, that she could now use to help others. In doing so, she had also discovered that her powers ranged much farther and wider than she had ever imagined.

With excitement Hannah ran into her bedroom, opened her closet, and grabbed for her dress. It was floor-length, beautiful, and black velvet. She had told her aunt how much she loved the painting of her at the top of the stairs, so Jewelia arranged to have one made just like it for her. She'd been looking forward to wearing the dress for weeks, and this was the morning a portrait artist was coming to paint her very own portrait. Hannah could hardly wait.

Jezebelle had traveled back to her home, forever changed for the better from what she'd experienced.

She had seen beyond the illusion, the world's perception of her, and gained a new perspective of her own. Hannah had discovered her special connection with Ashlin's legacy, that she too could commune with books. Now the entire manor library was more accessible than ever, just waiting for her. She could now learn so much, so fast.

Jewelia had asked Wendy to stay on permanently as the Skye Manor chef, a homage to her magickal culinary craft. While Maple Moon and her apartment were being repaired, Morgan also stayed at the manor, with Merlin and Milu at her side. The manor was so large, and there was plenty of room for everyone to live under the same roof and then some.

Late that evening, as the dark new moon rose in the sky, the women of Maple Hollow gathered around the table once more, surrounded by the abundance of the autumn harvest. Jewelia stood at the helm for an announcement.

"It is the final days before the Autumnal Equinox. Although we live in eternal autumn here in Maple Hollow, the rest of the world is now turning the wheel toward the darker half of the year. Now that we have embodied the light, it is time to usher in the darkness and embrace the shadows. Samhain is approaching fast. Dine with the spirits, my loves. They will guide you to embrace your true self."

They dined and drank to their hearts' delight. After the illustrious meal, they were served a final course by Old Man Adams. Each round, glowing dish was placed upon the dark mirror charger that waited at the bottom of the pile of plates. Wendy had concocted a liquid that both restored safety and confidence but also fortified one's own self-perception. She had given it to

Jezebelle as soon as she had stirred in her bed. As each woman drank from their cup, Morgan reminded them, "Beauty is to be yourself. Never forget you are one of a kind. There is power in your uniqueness. The outer world is merely a reflection of your inner world. Be the creatress of your universe. See through the illusion."

This time, when they stared into the darkness, every one of them saw their own inner beauty and wisdom. They were no longer held to the false visions of the shadow mirror, but instead could see through the illusion to their true selves. Surrounded by a sea of purple clouds that carried on its stream glistening stars, their faces beamed with smiles and their hearts lifted with hope. Gradually, they each became one with the fog, passing through their own mirror.

ACKNOWLEDGMENTS

I would like to send a heartfelt thanks to my family, friends, and fellow writers who have supported me on my author journey: my talented narrator Pearl Hewitt; my expert editing team and gifted book cover designer; my amazing podcast community; and all of the dedicated women in the Witches of Maple Hollow Team who champion my novels tirelessly with their creative efforts every day.

A Note to the Reader

Dear Reader,

I hope you've enjoyed the second book of the trilogy. If you'd like to be part of the Witches of Maple Hollow Community, I invite you to sign up for my newsletter, to receive magickal personal development and mystical guidance. I also hope you'll consider dropping a quick review at the retailer of your choice as well as on Goodreads. Continue your journey with Book 3, The Dream Dimensions!

I love to chat with other women who are intrigued by metaphysics and who wish to delve into the meaning of their dreams. Please reach out and share your experience—I'd love to hear it. Try my DreamMirror Method for yourself by downloading a free dream journal template at MeganMary.com and follow me @meganmaryauthor. Thank you again for your support.

Megan Mary

ABOUT THE AUTHOR

Metaphysical author Megan Mary, a dream analyst, intuitive, and mystic, intertwines her passion for personal transformation, magick, and cats with the ethereal realm of dreams.

In addition to a career spanning over twenty-five years creating, managing and marketing websites, she holds a BA and an MA in English Literature, certification in British Studies, is pursuing her PhD in Metaphysical Sciences, and is a member of the International Association for the Study of Dreams.

After being diagnosed with three chronic illnesses, she experienced a spiritual awakening. She now empowers women all over the world to live more authentic, aligned, and abundant lives through dream empowerment and mystical guidance. Her podcast, Women's Dream Enlightenment, has been voted as one of the Top 20 Spiritual Awakening Podcasts You Must Follow. When she's not dreaming or weaving digital webs, she enjoys spending time with her husband and two magickal cats.

Follow @MeganMaryAuthor on Instagram, Threads, YouTube, Pinterest, X & TikTok

Follow @MeganMaryAuthor on Instagram, Threads, YouTube, Pinterest, X & TikTok

www.ingramcontent.com/pod-product-compliance
Lightning Source LLC
Chambersburg PA
CBHW030140010826
48973CB00002B/656